05-09

A DEADLY WEAPON

The Piegan made no attempt to employ his bow. He had no need. Clutched in his right hand was a wicked weapon known as an eyedagg, a short club boasting a tapered spike at the end. It could shear into an eye socket clear to the brainpan.

Nate King's shoulder slammed into the Piegan's and both fell. Nate tried to twist to wind up on top but his leg caught on the man's war horse. Both of them landed on their sides. Heaving erect, Nate parried a blow aimed at his head. The heavy club jarred his forearm to the bone.

Circling, the Piegan swung again and again. Nate dodged, ducked, pivoted, all the while retreating. The club gave the warrior a greater reach, and it was all Nate could do to ward the flurry off.

Around them guns boomed, someone cursed, warriors screeched. Yet Nate dared not take his eyes off his adversary, not for a second, or that eyedagg would find a fatal spot. Once more he blocked a powerful swing to the head, the tip of the spike digging a tiny furrow into his cheek.

WILDERNESS

#24

Mountain Madness

←————————→

David Thompson

LEISURE BOOKS NEW YORK CITY

To Judy, Joshua, and Shane.

A LEISURE BOOK®

June 1998

Published by

Dorchester Publishing Co., Inc.
276 Fifth Avenue
New York, NY 10001

ISBN 0-8439-4399-8

Printed in the United States of America.

Mountain Madness

Chapter One

They were gong to die. They just knew it.

Isaiah Tompkins and Rufus Stern staggered westward under the hot summer sun. On all sides a sea of grass rustled dryly, fanned by a sluggish breeze. The two men walked with their heads bowed, their shoulders slumped. Neither noticed when a pair of coyotes rose from hiding to study them and then padded noiselessly away.

"We were fools," Isaiah declared bitterly. "We never should have left New York." He did not bring up the fact that the idea to get rich quick had been his. Which made him to blame if they died there in the middle of nowhere. He did not say it, but he thought it, and felt twice as bitter.

Rufus licked his dry lips. His mouth and throat were painfully sore. He did not want to talk, but he knew if he did not say something, his friend would sink deeper into the depths of despair. "Others have done it and succeeded."

"I don't see how."

They had both heard the stories of how scores of bold young

men had ventured beyond the frontier. Across the wide Mississippi to the vast prairie some called the Great American Desert, then beyond, to the fabled Rocky Mountains. Where peaks that glistened white with snow the year round towered miles into the sky. Where humpbacked bears bigger than horses prowled in constant hunger. Where painted savages lurked, waiting to slit the throats of the unwary.

What had most interested Isaiah and Rufus, though, were the tales about the trappers. Hardy souls who braved daily perils to reap thousands of dollars in bounty for beaver skins. It was said that beaver were as abundant as rabbits. All a man had to do was walk along a stream and pluck them out of the water as a child might pluck daisies.

Why, in a single trapping season, or so the accounts went, a man could earn upward of two thousand dollars. This, in a day when the average laborer was lucky if he earned four hundred a year. All it would take, Isaiah and Rufus had calculated, were five or six successful seasons and they could return to New York City with their pockets bulging with money.

Their loved ones argued against it. "Think of the dangers!" many had said. Parents, sisters, brothers, and others had all pointed out that there were plenty of good jobs to be had at home. Rufus's father had even offered to take them into his clothing business.

But Isaiah and Rufus would not be denied. Their heads swimming with visions of more money than either had ever seen in their entire lives, they combined their meager savings and bought what they felt they would need.

"Westward! To the Rockies!" Isaiah had cried on that fateful day they left. Now here they were many weeks later, stumbling wearily along, exhausted, starving, on the verge of collapse.

Gone were their mounts, their packhorses. All their supplies. Everything except the clothes on their backs, the heavy rifles in their hands, and their ammo pouches and powder horns.

Isaiah did not like to dwell on dying. He had to admit, though, that barring a miracle neither of them would live to see another sunset. It had been five days since they ate last. Almost three since they had a sip of water.

"I'll miss Agnes," Rufus commented sadly.

A twinge of conscience spiked Isaiah. Agnes Weatherby had been Rufus's betrothed. Of all their loved ones she had most resented their leaving. As well she should. Rufus had postponed the wedding in order to go along.

"I'll miss the theater, the nightlife," Isaiah said. *And the women.* A rake and a lady's man, he could never get enough of the opposite sex. His friends liked to joke he was addicted to them. And there were a bevy of beauties who could attest to his carnal cravings.

One of his fondest memories was the night he took Claire Beaumont to the Bowery Theater to see Madame Francisquay Hutin, a famed French dancer. Madame Hutin had bounded onto the stage wearing a short, semitransparent garment that had scandalized half the women in the audience into walking out. Claire, though, had stayed, and for some reason later had thrown herself at him in wild abandon. *How sweet that night had been!*

And how ironic, Isaiah mused, he should now regret his decision to leave New York when only a few short months ago he had craved to escape the bustling city, to strike out on a "grand adventure," to leave the past behind in order to finance the future.

"I am a dolt," Isaiah criticized himself, and did not realize he had spoken aloud until Rufus responded.

"Makes two of us. I could have backed out, but I didn't." Rufus paused to try to swallow. "I'm as much at fault as you."

They fell silent, too spent to waste energy talking. Isaiah willed his feet to keep shuffling, even though his legs protested

9

every step. He tried not to dwell on how hopeless their situation was.

Lacking food and water was bad enough. But they had no idea where they were. Yes, they were somewhere in the vast prairie, but exactly *where* eluded them. They had no inkling of how far off the mountains lay, and the mountains were their only hope of survival. There they'd find game in abundance, find streams and rivers where they could quench their thirst to their heart's content.

Squinting up at the afternoon sun, Isaiah wiped a sleeve across the sweat beading his brow. The hat he had purchased in New York—"guaranteed to hold up for years under the most adverse weather conditions"—hung limply down around his ears. The first rainstorm they encountered had about ruined the thing.

It had been the same with the rest of their provisions. Nothing held up as it should have. Clothes supposed to last a lifetime had frayed in no time. Their boots—"the most rugged and durable ever constructed"—were cracked and split and would soon fall apart.

It's this damnable wilderness, Isaiah thought. Blistering hot during the day, bone-chilling at night. Harsh winds that swept out of nowhere. Storms that pounded man and beast into the ground. And the lightning! How did one describe the vivid bolts raining out of the heavens? One after the other, so many they lit up the sky as brightly as midday, crackling and booming in a deafening din. One, in fact, had killed their best packhorse, charring the poor brute in its tracks.

Movement roused Isaiah out of his daze. At the limits of his vision animals moved.

More of those slender antelope he had seen before. Automatically he started to raise his rifle, then decided not to waste the effort. They never came within range, and whenever Rufus and he tried to sneak close enough for a shot, the antelope always streaked away in magnificent leaps.

Deer were no easier to slay. Again and again the two of them tried to shoot one; again and again the wily creatures had fled unscathed.

Small wonder Isaiah and Rufus were starving. Neither had done much hunting before they trekked westward. Until they reached the Mississippi it hadn't posed much of a problem, since there were taverns and inns galore to stop at each night. And once beyond the river, they had counted on their carefully hoarded supplies to see them through.

But the supplies were gone, along with the rest of their horses—which in itself was a major mystery. Isaiah was sure he had tethered the animals securely, as an innkeeper had advised. Yet one morning all six had been gone, with no clue to what happened. Even the tether rope had vanished.

Rufus was of the opinion the horses had somehow tugged free and wandered off. Isaiah was inclined to blame sinister forces. He was sure a smudged print he had found was part of a track left by a red heathen.

"I don't want to die," Rufus suddenly announced.

"No one in their right mind does," Isaiah replied.

"No, you misunderstand. I *really* want to live. I want to see my mother and father again. I want to hold Agnes in my arms and tell her how sorry I am for being such a fool."

Agnes again. "I owe her an apology too," Isaiah said. "If we ever make it back, I'll get down on bended knee and beg her forgiveness."

Rufus doubted it would do any good, but he held his tongue. He had never told Isaiah that Agnes despised him. She would never forgive Isaiah for luring him away. Rufus had lost count of how many times she broke into tears during the final weeks of preparation.

"I just can't understand you," she had sobbed on more than one occasion. "Leaving me alone. Going off to God-knows-where. And for what? Isaiah's silly dream. So what if you come back five thousands dollars richer? I would rather have

11

you than any amount of money in the world."

Always, she had clutched him, pleading, "Please don't go. For my sake. I'm begging you to stay. We'll marry and be together the rest of our lives. As it ought to be. Please say you won't go. Please!"

And always, Rufus sorrowfully recalled, he had pried her fingers loose, kissed her, and smugly told her not to worry. "Everything will be fine. You'll see. A year from now we'll have enough to buy our own house. Think how wonderful that will be."

Agnes would only sob louder.

Now Rufus forlornly gazed out over the unending plain. *I should have listened to you, sweet Agnes*, he reflected. *I am sorry for being such a dunderhead, for always thinking I knew best.*

An unexpected rumbling grunt brought Rufus and Isaiah to a stop. From out of the high grass on their left rose an ominous dark shape. A massive form, dense and shaggy, with a great wedge-shaped head crowned by wicked curved horns. It grunted again and swung toward them, its short tail twitching.

"A buffalo!" Isaiah blurted.

They had come on their first herd a few days west of the Mississippi, a small bunch that fled at their approach. Later, of course, they encountered much larger herds, some so immense it took a full day for the ungainly brutes to file by. Having heard lurid reports of men being fatally gored and trampled, they wisely stayed clear.

Still later, while in search of game, Rufus had stumbled on a cow and a calf. The mother had charged without warning. Rufus, safely mounted, easily escaped.

But now they were on foot. And the enormous bull glaring at them was less than ten yards away. It had risen from a wallow, a broad circular depression worn by constant rubbing and rolling.

"Do we shoot?" Rufus breathlessly asked.

"No." Isaiah had been told buffalo skulls were so thick, bullets bounced off. Striking a vital organ would be hard for a marksman, and they were fair shots at best. "Be still," he whispered, "and maybe it will let us be."

Rufus prayed his friend was right. Images of lovely Agnes paraded through his mind. If the time had come to meet his Maker, he wanted his last thoughts to be of her. "Yea, though I walk through the valley of the shadow of death," he intoned, "I will fear no evil."

"Hush," Isaiah warned. The bull had snorted and taken a step forward. It would not take much to provoke the monster.

Rufus wouldn't heed. "For Thou art with me. Thy rod and Thy staff, they comfort me. Thou preparest a table before me in the presence of mine enemies. Thou anointest my head with oil. My cup runneth—"

"Shush, in the name of all that's holy," Isaiah demanded, but the harm had been done.

Uttering an irate bellow, the gigantic bull lowered its head and attacked. It did not paw at the ground or toss its head. It did not give them an instant's forewarning of its intention, as a wayfarer at a tavern had assured Isaiah was always the case. No, it simply charged, exploding out of the wallow like a cannonball out of a cannon. Close to two thousand pounds of corded sinew propelled it with dazzling speed. In the blink of an eye it was on them.

Isaiah threw himself to the right. He fully expected to be smashed by that awful head. To be plowed under by heavy, hammering hooves. So he was pleasantly relieved when he hit on his shoulder and rolled up into a crouch, unhurt.

Rufus was not so quick—or so fortunate. He tried to dive to the right, but in his weakened state his unsteady legs would not cooperate. In midair he was jolted by an impact that whooshed the breath from his lungs. Sky and grass changed positions. He tumbled, wincing when he crashed onto the hard ground. Exquisite pain flared up his right leg, nearly swamping his consciousness.

The world spun. A murky veil sought to shroud Rufus, but he cast it off with a vigorous shake. He was flat on his back, pillowy clouds floating above. Muted drumming reminded him of the buffalo.

Thinking he was about to be attacked again, Rufus rolled onto his left side to push erect. A wave of pain struck, and once more the world danced crazily. Nausea afflicted him. Swallowing sour bile, he tried to gain his knees, but his left leg was racked by torment so overwhelming he nearly cried out.

Isaiah rushed over, his rifle extended, prepared to preserve his friend's life at the expense of his own if need be. But the bull was through with them. It had paid them back for daring to disturb it and was trotting toward the southern horizon.

Where there was one, though, there might be more. Isaiah looped an arm around Rufus's shoulders and lifted. "Come on. Let's keep going."

Rufus would have liked nothing better, but when he tried to stand, his left leg would not bear his weight. Raw agony doubled him over. If not for Isaiah he would have pitched onto his face. "My leg," he said. "I think it's broken."

Isaiah gamely braced Rufus against his side and hastened westward, casting repeated glances at the grass, fearful of another huge shape materializing. He tried not to think of the consequences. On foot—and healthy—they barely stood a prayer. With Rufus stricken, they would never reach the mountains. They would weaken further and die. As simple as that.

Rufus noticed that his ribs were sore to the touch. When he took deep breaths, several lower down hurt tremendously. He suspected one was cracked or broken, but he did not say so. A busted limb was enough to worry about. Head bent, he gritted his teeth and struggled to hold his own.

Isaiah was so worried about being set upon from the rear

or the sides that he did not pay much attention to what was in front of them. Another step, and the earth abruptly fell away. Too late, he saw that he had blundered onto another wallow. Gravity seized him, and he fell. He flung an arm out, but it was no use.

An outcry was torn from Rufus. Ribs and leg combined in an onslaught of sheer torture. Again he wound up on his back, dazed. And in no hurry to stand. He hurt too much. Propping himself on his elbows, he scrunched his nose in disgust at the awful reek of urine.

Isaiah reclaimed his rifle, then Rufus's. Except for the buzz of flies the prairie was quiet. "I don't think there are any other buffalo close by."

"Lucky for us," Rufus commented. Their first bit of luck in a blue moon. "Although I wouldn't mind a thick, juicy slab of roasted meat right about now."

Isaiah's stomach growled. "Don't remind me." Thinking about food only aggravated their plight. "Let's take a look at that leg." As he sank down, he heard a distant sound, one he assumed had been made by the buffalo.

Rufus levered high enough to sit up. His left side throbbed. His leg was infinitely worse. "Without a splint I won't be able to go half a mile."

"First things first. Roll up your pant leg." Isaiah did not point out they had not seen a tree in days. A splint was out of the question.

The brown pants Rufus had bought in New York were grimy, faded, and frayed at the bottom. Fabric guaranteed to last ten years had not lasted ten weeks. Gingerly, he pried at the hem, rolling it upward, afraid of what he would find. He did not understand when Isaiah suddenly gripped his wrist. "What's wrong?"

"Listen."

Rufus did, and heard nothing out of the ordinary. About to continue hiking the hem, he froze at the unmistakable faint nicker of a horse. To the southwest. "We're saved!" he exclaimed. "Maybe it's one of ours."

"Unlikely." Isaiah half rose, then thought better of exposing himself.

"White men, I'll bet. Let's give a shout to attract them."

"Hold on. What if it's not?" Isaiah's skin prickled as if from a heat rash. "Remember what that old fellow in St. Louis told us? Indians like to hunt buffalo." He paused. "What if it's a savage? Or an entire hunting party?"

Rufus's short-lived elation shattered on the jagged rocks of cruel reality. So far Fate had spared them from hostiles. They were long overdue to run into some. "Take a gander and tell me what you see."

Isaiah crept to the top. Flattening, he parted some grass. A pair of riders were heading in the wallow's general direction. As yet they were not close enough for him to note much detail other than the buckskins they wore and the white feather jutting from the head of the tallest. *A feather!* Isaiah slid down to Rufus and seized him by the arm. "I was right. Indians. We have to get out of here."

Rufus balked. If they had to make a stand, the wallow was the best spot they were likely to find. About nine feet in diameter and a foot or so deep, it offered more protection than the open prairie. He explained as much.

Reluctantly, Isaiah agreed. His foremost impulse was to run and keep on running until they were safe. But he would never desert Rufus, no matter what. "I'll help you to the top. Shoot anything that moves."

"What if they're peaceful?"

"Can we afford to take the chance?" Isaiah strained to keep his boyhood chum upright. "If they're friendly, they'll let us be. If they're not, they'll try to get in close to use their bows and lances. Be ready for anything."

Rufus felt there was a flaw in his partner's logic, but in his befuddled state he could not quite say what it was. Racked by pangs in his torso and his leg, he was grateful when they came to the crest so he could lie down.

Isaiah peered out. Dismay beset him on discovering the horses were in plain sight but the riders were nowhere to be seen. The men had dismounted, leaving the reins to dangle. "They're sneaking up on us," he whispered.

"How do you know?"

"Why else did they leave their animals out there and come on afoot?" Isaiah fingered the trigger of his rifle. "Don't fire until you have a sure shot. We can't afford to waste lead."

Rufus agreed. All their spare ammunition and powder had disappeared when the horses did. For which Isaiah couldn't blame him. Not when he had strongly suggested his friend remove the packs from the packhorses before turning in that night. He couldn't help it if he had been too tired to do the chore himself.

Each of them had about twenty balls left in his ammo pouch. Once that was gone they must resort to their long butcher knives. Hardly an appealing prospect.

A haze made the grass shimmer as if it were a reflection in a warped mirror. Rufus scoured the area without spotting the warriors. Apprehension tingled his spine as he imagined them snaking toward the wallow. He'd never fought an Indian before. He'd never fought anyone, in fact. So he couldn't honestly say if he had the courage to confront one in mortal combat, let alone actually take the life of another human being.

Judging by the lurid stories he'd heard during their travels, Rufus was glad he'd never had to find out. Harrowing tavern tales of captured whites skinned alive, of mountaineers who were scalped and lived to tell of it, of frontiersmen like Colter and others who had been made to run vicious gauntlets in order to save their skins.

Indians committed brutal acts. Everyone knew that. Many claimed it was because the red race was barely a notch above wild beasts in the overall scheme of things. While Rufus wasn't sure he would go that far, he was nonetheless petrified at the prospect of clashing with the warriors.

He glanced at Isaiah, who was scanning the prairie. Rufus wondered what his friend was thinking, if maybe Isaiah shared his sentiments.

At that exact instant, the other New Yorker was cursing himself for being stupid enough to think reaping a bonanza in beaver furs would be as easy as picking ripe cherries from a tree. Absently, he brushed a hand against his shirt. Under it was his dog-eared copy of *The Trapper's Guide* by Sewell Newhouse. It, more than anything else, was responsible for firing his imagination with dreams of being a trapper.

To those who were "looking out for pleasant work and ways of making" a lot of money, the *Guide* claimed to contain all the essential information anyone needed. Crucial provisions were listed in detail, along with tips on how to trap.

What the manual had *not* fully detailed, however, were the countless hardships. No mention of the unending trek across the Great American Desert, of the horrible storms, the lack of food and water. Isaiah wondered what else the manual didn't include.

Stirring grass brought Isaiah's musing to an end. Stems had rustled as if to the passage of a slinking form. Isaiah sighted down his rifle and applied his thumb to the hammer. Tense seconds expanded into a minute of anxious anticipation. When no one appeared, Isaiah relaxed a smidgen. Maybe he was jumping to conclusions, he tried to assure himself. Maybe the Indians were merely curious.

Rufus was gnawing on his upper lip, on a mustache that had sprouted over the past fortnight. Initially he had shaved every morning, just as he had done at the start of each day in New York. The scarcity of water put a stop to the habit. Now he had the mustache plus stubbly growth on his chin. Dear Agnes would hardly recognize him.

He also had hair well down past his ears. Since hostiles

were partial to lifting the hair of enemies, Rufus could not help but shudder at a gruesome mental image of his blood-stained scalp hanging from a peg in an Indian hovel. He couldn't let that happen. For Agnes's sake as well as his own.

"See anything?" Rufus whispered, and received a curt gesture in return.

Isaiah was annoyed his friend had been so careless. The hearing and eyesight of heathens were extraordinary, conditioned as they were by a lifetime of competing with wild creatures. Isaiah fretted the warriors had heard and pinpointed exactly where the wallow was, if they did not already know.

Rufus was upset. His friend could be rough on him on occasion, and it always stung. He would be the first to admit he wasn't necessarily the brightest individual who ever lived, but he always had their mutual best interests at heart. Hadn't he tagged along on Isaiah's grand adventure? What more proof could he offer of his undying friendship?

He became interested in the two horses. One was a splendid black stallion, the other an older white horse. The former grazed, the latter dozed. Rufus calculated the odds of reaching them before the Indians, but dismissed it as hopeless with his leg severely hurt.

Suddenly Rufus stiffened. A shadowy shape low to the ground had flitted briefly from west to east a dozen yards out. Elevating his rifle, he aligned the rear sight with the front sight as he had been taught, but by then the shape had melted into the earth. "Damn," he said to himself.

Isaiah heard, and frowned. Didn't his partner have a lick of common sense? Shifting to warn Rufus not to make the same mistake again, he ducked lower when something moved out among the thick stems. It had to be one of the Indians.

Just then, on the west side of the wallow, a loud thud sounded. Isaiah and Rufus both spun, bringing their weapons to bear. No one was there; they exchanged puzzled looks. It was Isaiah who spotted a rock lying on the wallow's slope, a rock that had not been present earlier. Its significance wasn't lost on him.

"Rufus! Look out!" Isaiah bawled, but the distraction had served its purpose.

Over the rim from opposite sides rushed two figures in buckskins, one springing at Isaiah, the other at Rufus.

Chapter Two

Isaiah Tompkins tried to bring his rifle to bear. Before he could, a pair of brawny arms encircled his chest and he was borne backward. For a brief instant he saw his assailant clearly and he was startled to his core. It was a white man, not an Indian. A tall, barrel-chested man with long black hair and a black beard. He also glimpsed a powder horn, ammo pouch, and large leather pouch slung crosswise, as well as a pair of pistols wedged under a wide brown leather belt.

Isaiah was so startled that when he struck the ground he made no move to defend himself. Which was just as well. Because in the time it would take a heart to beat, a pistol was pressed against the tip of his nose and a deep, resonant voice said, "Don't get your shackles up, hoss. This beaver feels like chawing, not making wolf meat of you." Isaiah wasn't quite sure he understood, but he made no attempt to resist.

Across the wallow, Rufus Stern had fared no better. He had not even begun to lift his rifle when the second attacker caught him across the shoulders in a tackle that left him flat on his back, rendered limp by anguish. It shocked Rufus to see the man was old enough to be his father. No, make that his *grandfather*. White hair and a bristly white beard framed a face crinkled by leathery wrinkles. Laughing blue eyes regarded him closely. "Pleased to make your acquaintance, young coon," the oldster said. "Don't be afraid." He leaned down and, incredibly, winked. "Remember what old William S. said."

"Huh?" was all Rufus could muster.

"Cowards die many times before their deaths. The valiant never taste of death but once. Of all the wonders that I yet have heard, it seems to me most strange that men should fear. Seeing that death, a necessary end, will come when it will come."

"Huh?" Rufus said again.

"The bard, son. Surely you've heard of Shakespeare?"

Rufus was not illiterate. He could read and write and knew a little about literature. Yes, he had heard of William Shakespeare, the English playwright. But to hear the bard being quoted by this white-haired apparition was bizarre beyond measure.

Isaiah Tompkins was no less astounded when the tall man who had pounced on him reached down and boosted him to his feet.

"No harm done, I reckon," said the giant, breaking into a smile. "The handle is Nate King. My pard and I were out hunting buffler when we spotted you. Sorry about sneaking up like we did, but we're not partial to lead between the eyes. And we know how skittish *mangeur de lards* can be."

"*Mangeur de* who?" Isaiah said in bewilderment.

"Greenhorns, pilgrim. Fresh from civilization. Like you and your friend, yonder." Nate King lowered the pistol and tucked it under his belt to the right of the big buckle. He was satisfied neither young man posed a threat.

Isaiah recovered his wits enough to ask, "Where did you

come from? Are you heading for the mountains to trap beaver?'' Something inside him seemed to snap, and his tongue wagged of its own accord. ''We're so glad to see you. We thought you were Indians. We've lost our horses and our supplies and my friend is hurt and we're just about on our last legs and—''

Nate King chuckled and raised a callused hand to quell the torrent. ''It's all right now. You're safe. We'll take you to my cabin. My family will love having company.''

''Cabin?'' Isaiah surveyed the plain. ''You live around here?''

Pointing westward, Nate said, ''Just a little ways off. Up in the mountains.''

Shakespeare McNair leaned closer to Rufus. ''Did I hear correctly, child? You've been hurt?''

Rufus was insulted. ''Just because I'm younger than you doesn't give you the right to call me that. I'm a grown man, damn it.''

''In the reproof of chance lies the true proof of men.''

''What?''

''The sea being smooth, how many shallow bauble boats dare sail upon her patient breast, making their way with those of nobler bulk! But let the ruffian Boreas once enrage the gentle Thetis, and anon behold the strong-ribb'd bark through liquid mountains cut, bounding between the two moist elements, like Perseus' horse. Where's then the saucy boat, whose weak untimber'd sides but even now co-rivall'd greatness?''

''Huh?''

Shakespeare peered intently at the younger man's hair. ''Were you knocked on the head? Is that why you're so addlepated?''

''I can't understand half of what you say, old man.''

Nate King roared with laughter as he came over. ''You're not the only one, stranger. I've been telling him that for years.

23

David Thompson

But what can you expect from a gent who totes around *The Complete Works of William Shakespeare* everywhere he goes?'' He lowered his voice as if confiding a secret. ''I'm partial to James Fenimore Cooper, myself.''

Isaiah shook his head. It was too ridiculous for words. He was half-tempted to pinch himself to verify he wasn't dreaming. Here, apparently, were two honest-to-goodness mountain men, the kind he had read about, men who lived in the wilderness year in and year out, who fought bears and Indians daily, who were supposed to be the hardiest souls alive. And what were they doing? Joshing about their favorite authors! ''I didn't think trappers liked to read,'' he lamely said.

Nate started up the wallow, saying over a shoulder, ''There's nothing like a good book during those long winter spells when the snow is higher than the cabin door.''

''In the old days us mountaineers would swap books all winter long,'' Shakespeare elaborated. ''We'd sit up past midnight discussing all the greats. Byron, Scott, Clark's Commentary, you name it.'' He brightened at the memory. ''The Rocky Mountain College, we called it. A man could get quite an education thataway.''

Rufus knew next to nothing about the others McNair had mentioned. Reading had always seemed like a waste of time to him. Why spend hours with his nose in a book when he could spend those same hours living life to the fullest? Not having anything to contribute, he said instead, ''I was attacked by a bull buffalo.''

Shakespeare turned serious. ''You don't say? Let's have a look.''

Rufus was going to say the man did not have to bother, but the oldster squatted and probed him from head to toe with the precision of a New York physician. He answered ''Yes!'' when McNair lightly pressed against his ribs, and again when the mountain man examined his left leg.

Isaiah, watching, did not realize Nate King had left until

24

the tall trapper returned bearing two rifles unlike any he had ever beheld. Shorter than his own, both were thicker and had elaborately decorated stocks. "Nice guns," he commented.

Nate wagged the pair. "Made by the brothers, themselves," he said, and proudly held one for Isaiah to read the capital letters engraved on the lockplate: J & S HAWKEN—ST. LOUIS.

Shakespeare rose, scratching his beard. "Well, our young friend here has a busted rib and a badly bruised leg, but he can ride."

"My leg isn't broken?" Rufus asked in some surprise.

"No way but gentleness. Gently, gently. The fiend is rough, and will not be roughly used."

"Pardon?"

"Go easy on that leg, Horatio. It's not busted, but you won't be playing hopscotch for a week or so." Shakespeare accepted his Hawken from Nate. "I'll fetch the horses. Won't Winona be surprised when we show up? What with her kin visiting and all." Chortling, he scampered off.

Nate King did not share his friend's glee. Studying the two greenhorns, he wondered if he was making a mistake in taking them to his home. How would they react once they arrived? Were they decent at heart? So many whites harbored mindless hate born of ignorance.

"Who is Winona?" Isaiah asked.

"My wife." Nate changed the subject. "I don't recollect hearing who you are, mister. Or what brings you to this corner of the world."

Isaiah corrected his oversight. Briefly, he explained about his dream to be a beaver trapper and was puzzled when King gave him a peculiar look. "Now, of course, our dream is ruined," he concluded. "Without horses and provisions, we have no choice but to somehow make our way back to St. Louis." He hesitated, reluctant to ask someone he did not know for aid. For Rufus's sake, he added, "Any help you can give us will be greatly appreciated."

"You'll be taken care of, don't fret." Nate walked to the rim to await Shakespeare and to ponder. Tompkins and Stern had no notion of how fortunate they were. Countless well-meaning but foolish men just like them had paid a fatal price for their folly. It was just dumb luck that McNair and he had happened on the pair when they did.

Nate sighed and reached up to adjust the eagle feather adorning his hair. Not more than three moons ago he had been out on the prairie hunting and stumbled on a collection of bones and moldy store-bought clothes.

A yellowed journal, warped and discolored but still partly legible, had recorded the final thoughts of a would-be trapper from Ohio. A youth who had struck out on his own and suffered a fate similar to that of the New Yorkers.

Indians, most likely Pawnees or Lakotas, had stolen the youth's horses and his possibles. He had pressed on in the forlorn hope of reaching the Rockies, but died of starvation. The last journal entry had been a plea. A request scribbled to anyone who might find his remains. Would they please find a way of getting the journal to his kin? he had begged. To his ma and pa and sister.

Nate had mulled it over and finally sent the journal back with a party of mountain men bound for St. Louis. It might lessen the family's torment. Knowing the youth's fate was better than not knowing. Wasn't it?

Shakespeare trotted up, leading Nate's big black stallion. Glancing at the would-be trappers, he said so only Nate could hear, "Are you sure about this, hoss? I can take them to my cabin instead."

"In the shape they're in? No, you live a lot farther away."

"Suit yourself." McNair grinned. "Weigh what convenience both of time and means may fit us to our shape. If this should fail, and that our drift look through our bad performance, 'Twere better not assay'd. Therefore, this project should have a back or second, that might hold if this did blast in proof.''

"Translation?"

"If the worst comes to pass I'll take them on to my cabin anyway. Blue Water Woman won't mind. Too much." Shakespeare dismounted and said to the greenhorns, "Let's light a shuck. You boys get to ride double on Pegasus. Nate's horse tends to act up if someone it doesn't know tries to climb on."

Isaiah snickered. "You named your horse after that Greek myth?"

Shakespeare gave his animal an affectionate rub. "All he's missing are the wings. And when he was younger, you'd have sworn he had a pair. He flew like the wind. Wasn't a horse alive could catch him. Why, once Nate and me were over the Divide when a band of Utes swept down, chasing us for plumb near fifty miles—"

"It was more like five," Nate amended, and nudged his mentor. "Help me lift Rufus on Pegasus, then you can jabber us to death."

"Jabber?" Shakespeare drew himself up to his full height. "Say what you will, my sweet Hamlet, but one thing I never do is *jabber*." Jaw jutting, he made for Rufus and Isaiah. As he squatted to assist Rufus in standing, he thrust a thumb at Nate and whispered, "Here's Agamemnon. An honest fellow enough, and one that loves quails. But he has not so much brain as earwax."

Isaiah burst into peals of mirth. He couldn't help himself. Not after the nightmare he had been through, after believing he was doomed, believing his time among the living could be measured in days rather than years. That awful certainty had gnawed at his soul for hours on end. Then—to be abruptly saved by so comical a character triggered a flood of laughter he couldn't stop if he wanted. All the emotions he had pent up, all the frustration and heartbreak and fear, gushed from him in rowdy, joyous laughs.

Shakespeare joined in, thinking his jest was responsible. Soon it was obvious something else was. Stopping, he scrutinized the New Yorker to determine if maybe, just maybe, the man suffered from too much sun.

Nate King was glad when they were finally under way. After sharing water from a water skin and a handful of pemmican apiece, they climbed into the saddle. Nate rode double with McNair, the big stallion showing no strain at having to bear their combined weight.

Isaiah had been under the impression the mountain man's cabin was close by. Yet the prairie extended to the west for as far as the eye could see. "Didn't you say you live in the high country?"

"In the prettiest little valley in all Creation," Nate confirmed.

"Will it take long to reach it?"

"It's just a short piece. You'll see. We'll be there before you know it," Nate assured him.

Mile after mile fell behind them. Presently a bloodred sun perched on the brink of the world, banding the heavens with bright pink, orange, and yellow hues. "Lord, I never tire of the sunsets out here," Isaiah mentioned.

Neither had Nate. Not even after living in the wild a good fifteen winters. Sunsets, sunrises, each and every day was precious. No two were ever alike. Unlike the days during his fledgling career as an accountant, when drudgery had been the norm and boredom had been routine.

Slavery, pure and simple. That was what city life amounted to. Getting up every morning at the crack of dawn to eat a bland breakfast and then trek off to work, filing along the same narrow streets, passing the same tightly packed buildings, to sit at a small desk in a crowded room and spend ten to twelve hectic hours scrawling tiny figures in thinly spaced ledgers.

And for what? A pittance. For barely enough money to scrape by. Adding insult to injury, he'd had to abide the abuse of a cranky employer, a boss who delighted in nitpicking. A skinflint who was not above carping about every flaw his workers had but could never condescend to compliment those who did their jobs well.

How many untold thousands had to put up with the same daily drudgery? How many millions? Nate had heard tell that some of the bigger cities, bustling places like New York and Philadelphia and Boston, were now so crammed that people couldn't walk down a street without bumping elbows. Even worse, sections were unfit for decent folks to be in at any time of the day or night. Fallen women, footpads, charlatans, and murderers were as common as fleas on a coonhound.

Nate never regretted leaving the city for the wilderness. He had traded slavery for freedom. From being totally dependent on others, he had come full circle and was now dependent on no one except himself. And his wife, naturally. She was as much a part of him as the air he breathed, as the blood coursing through his veins.

Winona. Nate never stopped marveling at the depth of their love. Or at how their love had grown over the years, mushrooming from the first heady rush of raw lust lovers always experienced into the mature love adults shared.

It was downright strange how men and women were so different yet so alike. Strange how they spatted like cats and dogs, yet couldn't live without one another. Strange how each complemented the other. How even their bodies had been designed by a Higher Hand to match perfectly, to fit snugly, as it were.

At a rendezvous Nate had listened to a blowhard say that females were the bane of existence, that no man worthy of the name would shackle himself to one. The simpleton had deserved a rap on the noggin with a rock, but Nate had refrained.

Some men were too vain or selfish or stupid to see the point.

David Thompson

Being in love wasn't the same as being in bondage. True love was not forged from chains but from the furnace of passion and desire mixed with a deep sense of need. Need that surpassed all human understanding.

His need for Winona was a prime example. He could no more live without her than he could without his own heart. Years ago, shortly after they were joined as husband and wife, she had confided her belief that the Great Mystery had brought them together. That their meeting was foreordained. That they had been destined to be together from the day they were born. Possibly before.

He had laughed, dismissing it as a flight of female fancy. But as time went by, as their affection grew into an unbreakable bond, as he saw how perfect a match they were, he had come to think that maybe, just maybe, she was right.

Their bond had seen them through many a hardship. It was his hope, his prayer, that it would see them through many more. Including the major inconvenience he was about to inflict on her.

As if to remind the trapper of the gamble he was taking, Isaiah Tompkins picked that moment to declare, "That feather you wear almost got your head shot off, King. I mistook you for an Indian."

Rufus was leaning against his partner, his jaw muscles clenched. "Why do you wear that silly thing, anyhow?" he wanted to know.

Nate held in check a fleeting surge of resentment. "It was a gift long ago from a Cheyenne warrior. A token of friendship. I value it highly."

Isaiah's interest was piqued. Rumor had it that some of the wilder mountaineers, those more animal in nature, mingled with various heathens from time to time. "Have you ever lived with the Cheyennes?"

"No. With the Shoshones, my adopted people. And with the Flatheads, who took Shakespeare into their tribe. A few

30

times I've stayed overnight with the Crows. And once or twice with the Utes.''

Isaiah was flabbergasted. ''Am I to understand that a tribe of heathens actually *adopted* you? Made you one of their own?''

Nate looked squarely into the New Yorker's eyes. ''Do yourself a favor. Don't call Indians heathens and I won't call you a bigoted son of a bitch. Fair enough?''

''Now, see here. Everyone knows Indians don't believe in the Bible. What else does that make them, if not heathens?''

Shakespeare came to Nate's defense. ''There are more things in heaven and earth, Horatio, than are dreamt of in your philosophy.''

''Meaning what, old man?''

''Meaning it's not wise to judge another's bushel by your own peck.'' Shakespeare clucked in disapproval. ''Didn't it ever occur to you that the God you worship is the same Great Mystery or Great Spirit or whatever you want to call it revered by most Indians?''

''Even if that's true, they're still not Christians. They know nothing of our Master, who is our salvation and our glory. He is the way, the truth, and the light, and without Him none of us will taste eternal life.''

''Bible-thumper, huh?'' Shakespeare pursed his lips. ''Even so, you can't blame the Indians for not being something they know nothing about. Until the first pilgrim set foot at Plymouth Rock, they had never even heard of the carpenter from Nazareth.''

Isaiah was about to say that was no excuse but changed his mind. The old-timer had a valid point.

Shakespeare pressed his advantage. ''Instead of branding all Indians as worthless trash or hopeless sinners, maybe you should keep in mind what Jesus himself said. 'The harvest truly is plentiful, but the laborers are few. Therefore pray the Lord of the harvest to send out laborers into His harvest.' ''

Isaiah was impressed. "You certainly know your Scripture."

"I've read the Bible from Genesis to Revelation, from 'In the beginning' to the final 'Amen.' "

"Yet you seem more partial to the works of Shakespeare."

"Old William S. makes me laugh. And Jesus himself said to always be of good cheer."

"Something tells me you're mixing apples and oranges, but I won't quibble. Nor will I think so harshly of Indians from now on. You've helped me to see them in a whole new light."

"Good. There's hope for you yet."

Nate was not so easily appeased. Too many whites and red men alike hated the other race for no other reason than the color of their skin. Often they pretended to be the best of friends but nursed their hatred in secret. He made a mental note to keep an eye on the pair the whole time they stayed at his homestead.

Rufus had another question to pose. "Did you say your wife's name was Winona? Never heard it before. Is she by any chance a squaw?"

The young man had no idea how close he came to being bashed in the face. If not for his weakened state, he would have paid, and paid dearly, for his brash insult. Nate faced due west and answered more gruffly than he intended, "Yes. She's Shoshone. What of it?"

"Nothing, nothing," Rufus said quickly. A bit too quickly. The big trapper's tone hinted he had somehow given offense, but he did not see how. Was it his use of the word *squaw*? he wondered. How could that be, when everyone did it?

Isaiah contentedly took another bite of the food Nate had given them and munched loudly, savoring the taste. "What is this stuff? It's delicious."

"Pemmican. My wife made it."

"What from?"

"Dry buffalo meat, ground up and mixed with berries and

fat. It's a favorite of the Shoshones and others. Lasts a long time. And it's nutritious.''

''Why have we never heard of this back in the States? A man could make a small fortune selling it.''

Shakespeare McNair replied, ''Haven't you noticed, young-ster? Most of what is written about Indians has to do with their so-called bad qualities. How savage they are. How they delight in raping and maiming. How they torture their enemies. Nothing is ever said of their good traits.''

''They have some?''

Shakespeare had to remind himself youth and stupidity went hand in hand. ''The evil that men do lives after them. The good is oft interred with their bones.'' He gave his beard a tug in mild exasperation. ''Let's take the Flatheads, since I know them best. They're always even-tempered, always friendly. Men and women alike are devoted parents. They frown on drunkenness. Murder is unknown. If you were to show up at one of their villages in the same state we found you in, the Flatheads would feed you and give you a lodge all to yourself. No strings attached.''

''Don't get me wrong,'' Isaiah said. ''I'm not saying all Indians are evil. I know my history. I know how the first Pilgrims were treated.''

The drone of voices was having an effect on Rufus. Lulled by a sense of security, with the trappers there to protect them, he was unable to keep his eyes open. Several times he dozed, losing track of the talk.

Nate King rested his Hawken across his thighs and took note of the western horizon. Before long the Rockies would hove into view, and the emerald-green foothills bordering them. Focused as he was to the west, he did not catch sight of the riders to the north until the stallion swung its head and pricked its ears. Instantly he slowed.

Shakespeare and Isaiah were still debating the good and bad traits of the red race. ''So we're agreed?'' the young man was saying. "There are some Indians it's best to avoid if you want to stay healthy."

"That there are," McNair conceded. "The Blackfeet and their allies, for starters. They'd as soon slit a white man's throat as look at him."

"Speak of the devil," Nate said, pointing. "Here come some now."

Chapter Three

Isaiah Tompkins was sure Nate King had to be joking. Hostile Indians would not ride right up to them in broad daylight. It was preposterous. Then Shakespeare McNair slid off Pegasus and stepped a few yards to the left, holding his Hawken with the barrel almost level. And Nate King loosened both pistols, then slanted his own Hawken so all he had to do was raise it an inch or so to shoot. Isaiah took his cue from them and tucked the stock of his long gun to his side, ready for use.

Rufus snored lightly. Isaiah twisted to wake him, but Shakespeare said, "Leave him be. The shape he's in, he wouldn't be of much help anyway."

"But an extra gun would come in handy," Isaiah said. He counted seven Indians, strung out in a row, riding with their mounts shoulder to shoulder. Since these were the first Indians he had encountered, with the exception of a few tame ones in St. Louis, he noted every little detail about them.

Their clothing was scanty. Breechcloths or loincloths for the most part, made from soft deer hide, Isaiah guessed. A few

35

had on buckskins. Their bodies were dark from long exposure to the sun. Isaiah was relieved to see that only one warrior possessed a rifle. The rest held bows. Not one had an arrow notched to a string, which was odd.

"Piegans," Nate King said. Along with the Bloods, they were part of the widely feared Blackfoot Confederacy, a loose association of three powerful tribes who controlled the northern plains and the lower part of Canada. "Usually we don't see them this far south."

"Are they really very dangerous?" Isaiah asked. "I mean, they don't look as if they want to cause trouble."

Shakespeare McNair snorted. "Don't let them fool you, youngster. They'll nock an arrow and let it fly before you can blink. Watch their hands, not their eyes. Their eyes won't give anything away. They lie through their teeth and never show it."

"Why are they riding up to us like this? Why don't they just attack?"

"They haven't quite made up their minds whether they want to jump us yet," Shakespeare speculated. "All we have are two horses. Not worth the bother if it costs them a life. So they're coming for a closer look. Everything will depend on whether they think they can lick us without losing one of their own."

The Piegans slowed when they were forty yards out and walked their mounts the rest of the way. Isaiah was surprised to find that overall, they had handsome, finely chiseled features. They weren't the ugly brutes he had been led to believe most savages were. Their black hair was long. A couple wore it loose over the shoulders. Others had braids. In the center rode a lean warrior from whose head rose porcupinelike quills. This man also had rings in his ears and a fine beaded necklace. Over his right shoulder was a short red blanket. Dark, crafty eyes gleamed with vitality. Something told Isaiah this was the one to watch, the one who would decide whether to fight or part in peace.

Nate King had reached the same conclusion. Focusing on the dandy, he waited until they were fifteen feet out, then declared, "That's close enough, Little Robe. What do you want?"

The Piegan's mouth creased in a sly smile. "Grizzly Killer. I hear maybe you dead. I very happy." His English was atrocious and badly accented, but understandable.

"Only believe half of what you see and a third of what you hear," Nate quipped.

Isaiah couldn't believe his own ears. "You know this barbarian personally?"

Little Robe's dark eyes narrowed with thinly veiled disgust. "Who this white dog be, Grizzly Killer?"

"Dog!" Isaiah bristled. "How dare you! I don't take kindly to insults, especially from crude clods like you." He shifted, his arms rising, then turned to marble when several of the warriors flashed hands to their quivers.

Shakespeare McNair advanced a few feet. "Hold your tongue, youngster," he cautioned. "Trading insults is a time-honored tradition out here. Little Robe hates us so much, he couldn't resist trading a few." He plastered a huge smile on his craggy face. "Isn't that right, you fish-eating bastard?"

Little Robe laughed, a brittle tinkle as icy as an arctic gale. "Funny, Carcajou. Like always, eh?" He made a show of inspecting McNair. "How you still live, old one? My father's father knew you when you no bigger my dog."

Shakespeare laughed. "Good one. I see you've been working on your sense of humor. First I ever knew you had any."

Isaiah was utterly confounded. It was as plain as the nose on his face that the mountain men and the Piegans were bitter enemies, yet they sat there trading barbs as nonchalant as you please.

It was Little Robe's turn to laugh. "Tell you, Carcajou. Day

I hang your hair my lodge, day I dance and sing.''

"Glad I'll be dead," Shakespeare bantered. "You can't hold a note worth spit."

Nate King kept his eyes on the others. They were tense, but not quite as tense as they should be. And each and every one of them was grinning, as if at some private joke. It couldn't be the exchange between McNair and Little Robe, because none of the other Piegans spoke a lick of English. Puzzled, Nate mulled the possible explanations and came to the only logical conclusion.

"Oh, you be dead, Carcajou," Little Robe said. "Be dead soon."

McNair hefted his Hawken. "Cuts both ways, hoss."

An itchy sensation erupted between Nate's shoulder blades. "Say, Shakespeare," he said casually. "What was the name of that play old William S. wrote about the Greeks?"

"Huh?" Genuinely taken aback, Shakespeare looked up at the man he considered more as a son than a friend. "Well, now. That's a real pertinent question, given the situation. Since when have you shown any interest in his masterpieces?"

"The Greek one," Nate emphasized. "Remember it?"

"William S. had Greeks in several. How should I know which one you're talking about?"

"Oh, you'll recall this one. About Troy, remember?"

"*Troilus and Cressida*. What about it?"

The itching grew worse. Nate resisted an impulse to turn and maintained a calm manner. "Remember the part where that Trojan warrior was in his tent? And what that Greek did?"

"Hector, you mean?" Shakespeare said, and suddenly insight seared him like a red-hot knife. Yes, he recollected it well. How the Greek Achilles had refused to meet Hector in mortal combat, then later snuck into Hector's tent when the Trojan was unarmed and had his men fall on Hector and hack him to death. "Though this be madness, yet there be method to it."

38

Little Robe was displeased. "What you talk about? Who these be?"

"Achilles was distant kin of yours," Shakespeare rejoined. "He had as much honor as you do. Which is to say, none whatsoever."

"Honor?" the Piegan repeated.

"Mine honor keeps the weather of my fate. Life every man holds dear, but the dear man hold honor far more precious-dear than life."

"Fah!" Little Robe spat. "You talk crazy talk. Like always."

Shakespeare edged toward the black stallion without being obvious. "No more crazy talk, enemy mine. From this moment on, the strand between us is severed. What happens next is on your shoulders, not mine. I'd have been content to let bygones be bygones."

"What is bygones?"

"Parting is such sweet sorrow," Shakespeare quoted, and cackled as if he truly were insane. As he cackled, he thrust his rifle up and out. Thumbing the hammer back, he sent a lead ball smack into the middle of Little Robe's forehead.

Simultaneously, Nate King whirled in the saddle. Four more Piegans were within bow range, creeping along doubled close to the ground, making no more noise than would four ethereal specters. The foremost was a husky warrior who had a barbed shaft nocked to a sinew string. Nate's shot cored the man's sternum.

It all happened so fast that Isaiah Tompkins was wreathed in swirling tendrils of acrid smoke before he quite understood what was happening. He saw Nate snatch out a pistol and fire again, even as Shakespeare unlimbered a flintlock and brought down a Piegan sighting down an arrow.

"Ride!" Nate bawled, and leaned down to smack Pegasus on the flank. The white horse bolted, nearly throwing Isaiah, who had to clutch the saddle in order to stay on.

Behind him, Rufus Stern was jolted awake by the blasts. Snapping upright, he blinked in confusion. "What's happening? What's going on?" The violent jerk Pegasus gave breaking into motion threw him backward, and in befuddled desperation he clawed at his friend, almost unhorsing Isaiah along with himself.

Shakespeare was in motion, too, moving remarkably spryly for someone his age. A bound took him to the stallion. Nate's free arm descended and hauled him up while at the same moment Nate applied his heels, goading the big black into pell-mell flight.

Arrows cleaved the air from both directions, buzzing like enraged bees. A shaft meant for the mountain men passed through the space Nate had just occupied, into the chest of the Piegan who had been on Little Robe's left. Confusion reigned. Milling, the warriors hollered at one another.

It bought Nate and Shakespeare the precious seconds they needed to gain a narrow lead. Swiftly, they overtook the New Yorkers, whose legs were flapping like those of disjointed rag dolls.

"Keep going due west!" Nate cried. "No matter what, don't stop!"

Isaiah had no intention of stopping. Not when five Indians were in full pursuit, yipping and howling like a pack of rabid dogs. The others were gathering around the bodies of the slain. From the southeast hastened two more on horseback, leading four other animals.

Isaiah put two and two together and realized the second group had been sneaking up on them the whole time, that Little Robe had intended to keep them talking until it was too late. How on earth Nate King had guessed, he was at a loss to say.

The stallion and the white horse were holding their own. But appearances were deceiving. Horses bearing double weight could never outdistance horses bearing one person.

Eventually both would tire and the Piegans would catch up.

Nate scoured the prairie, seeking a break in the flat terrain. There was none. No gullies, no washes, not a single coulee. To the southwest, though, rose what appeared to be a small bump. Distance and the heat haze were responsible for the illusion.

"Head there!" Nate said, and cut to the left.

Isaiah was a shade slow in reacting. A glittering shaft, whizzing out of the blue within an inch of his head, provided incentive to be more alert. Bending low, he galloped madly toward that far-off bump. What good it would do was beyond him. But if he had learned anything during his short association with the two mountaineers, it was to trust their judgment. Implicitly.

It soothed Isaiah somewhat that neither trapper betrayed so much as a hint of panic or fright. McNair even smiled as if he were enjoying himself immensely. But then, Isaiah had begun to suspect the oldster was a few marbles shy of a full bag. Why else would the old man go around quoting William Shakespeare every chance he got?

Unknown to the New Yorker, McNair *was* enjoying himself. The skirmish reminded him of his younger days, when seldom a week had gone by without a hair-raising escapade. In those days only a few whites roamed the mountains, mostly intrepid Frenchmen known as *voyageurs*. Some of the bravest men Shakespeare ever met. To call them fearless did not begin to do them justice. The *voyageurs* had gone where no white men before them had ever gone, exploring uncharted, untamed country that stretched from Canada to Mexico.

Then came the trappers. Beaver fur had become all the rage among the rich back east, and the rich always set fashion trends for everyone else. The price for beaver peltries shot up like a geyser, luring hundreds of dreamy-eyed men to the Rockies in pursuit of the dream at the end of their personal

41

rainbows. Only a handful ever emerged with the riches they sought.

Their coming forever changed the wilderness. Scattered trading posts and forts were erected. Indians learned to crave trade goods, luxuries they could never obtain otherwise. Rifles, pistols, steel knives and hatchets, Hudson's Bay blankets, tin pots and pans and so much more, became part and parcel of the Indian way of life.

As a result, the Indian way of life was forever transformed. Just as the horse, introduced by the Spanish, enabled Indians to rove far and wide and become lords of their domain, so the trade goods of the whites elevated their standard of living. But where before most Indians had been content to have enough buffalo meat to feed their families and a fine warhorse to use on raids, now they had to have all those wonderful things the whites did.

Indians weren't as self-sufficient as they had been in Shakespeare's younger days. Each year their addiction to simple luxuries made them more and more dependent on white men. And that saddened him. For there was bound to come a day when Indians wanted *everything* the whites had, and that would be the end of their culture and their freedom.

A war whoop prompted Shakespeare to save his musing for later. The Piegans were gaining. One in particular, astride a superb sorrel, had pulled well ahead and was within easy bow range. The man clamped his legs to the sorrel so his hands were free, then pulled his bow string back.

Shakespeare's Hawken was empty. It was impossible to reload bouncing on the back of the stallion. But the Piegan didn't know that. Snapping the rifle up, Shakespeare pretended to fix a bead.

The warrior had no hankering to die. Guiding the sorrel by his knees alone, he veered sharply to the right and dropped back a piece.

"Called your bluff!" Shakespeare yelled in impish glee.

The same trick might work once or twice, but soon the Piegans would guess the truth and spur their animals to greater speed.

Nate lashed the stallion to stay even with Pegasus. The small bump had grown in size, swelling to a height of ten to twelve feet and a width of twenty. An isolated knoll, the only cover to be had within miles. It would have to do. "How are you two holding up?" he shouted at the greenhorns.

"Just dandy!" Isaiah replied. Although he was scared to death and his heart was hammering as if on the verge of exploding, a perverse thrill animated him. A feeling of keen excitement, a feeling he enjoyed.

Rufus did not share his friend's outlook. His ribs were aflame and his left leg protested every loping stride the white horse took. In addition, his stomach was queasy, so queasy he was afraid he would be ill. He sagged against Isaiah, too weak to lift his rifle.

The war whoops rose in volume when the Piegans divined where the white men were headed. Two slanted to either side.

Shakespeare swiveled when a warrior to the north tried to cut them off. Again he raised his Hawken. Again the ruse worked. Another minute and they would be at the knoll. Then it would be root hog or die.

The Piegans were converging. They had lost the race, so their only hope to avoid a standoff was to overwhelm the whites in a concerted rush. Screeching like banshees, they bore down on their quarry.

Nate still had one pistol loaded and primed. He snatched it as he rounded the knoll and reined up in a spray of dust. Vaulting off, he ran toward the top, halting midway to train the flintlock on the Piegan on the sorrel. Immediately the warrior slanted wide and dropped from sight on the opposite side of his animal, displaying only a heel and an elbow.

Shakespeare had jumped down and was running to the right. A pair of warriors were closing in, arrows notched. Yanking out his second pistol, he fired as the shafts zinged clear of the bows. Then he flung himself sideways. He heard a thud at his feet and a searing twinge in his shoulder. With all three guns empty, he had no recourse but to grab his butcher knife and rise to meet the Piegans head-on. There was no time to reload.

Isaiah had clambered from Pegasus. He rotated on the balls of his feet, then dashed several yards up the incline and saw McNair's predicament. Hastily lining up his barrel on one of the warriors, he fired.

By a sheer fluke the ball struck the man's temple, lifted him clean off his horse, and pitched him into the second Piegan, who tried to rein clear. Both the dead warrior and his companion were unhorsed, pitching roughly to the soil some forty feet out.

Shakespeare dropped onto his knees, uncapped his powder horn, and set to reloading.

Rufus Stern was still on the white gelding. Overcome by dizziness, he plopped onto its back, his arms dangling, his rifle slowly slipping from fingers going limp. He craved nothing more than lots and lots of uninterrupted sleep. Twenty hours or more and he would feel like a new person.

Suddenly Pegasus shied. Rufus sluggishly raised his head and was amazed to see that a Piegan had picked him as a likely victim. The Indian was going to ride right into the gelding. Rufus sat up quickly, lost his grip on the rifle, and listened to it clatter. Feral triumph lit the bronzed features of the warrior.

The Piegan made no attempt to employ his bow. He had no need. Clutched in his right hand was a wicked weapon known as an "eyedagg," a short club boasting a tapered spike at the end. It could shear into an eye socket clear to the brainpan.

On the knoll, Nate King saw what was happening and banged off a hasty shot that missed. Casting the pistol and his rifle down, he rushed to intercept the Piegan. The warrior was almost on top of Stern when Nate palmed his knife and leaped.

The trapper's shoulder slammed into the Piegan's, and both

men fell. Nate tried to twist to wind up on top, but his leg caught on the man's warhorse. Both of them landed on their sides. Heaving erect, Nate parried a blow aimed at his head. The heavy club jarred his forearm to the bone.

Circling, the Piegan swung again and again. Nate dodged, ducked, pivoted, all the while retreating. The club gave the warrior a greater reach, and it was all Nate could do to ward the flurry off.

Around them guns boomed, someone cursed, warriors screeched. Yet Nate dared not take his eyes off his adversary, not for a second, or that eyedagg would find a fatal spot. Once more he blocked a powerful swing to the head, the tip of the spike digging a tiny furrow in his cheek.

In all the confusion Nate bumped into a horse. He could not say which. It brought him up short. The warrior exploited the moment by sidestepping, then driving the eyedagg at Nate's midsection. Nate lowered his empty hand, seizing the eyedagg's shaft. He tried to thrust his knife into the man's groin, but the Piegan grasped his wrist.

Locked together, they strained. The mountain man was larger, but the warrior was as strong as a bull. Neither could gain an advantage. The Piegan flung out a foot, then jerked around, seeking to trip his foe.

Nate imitated a jackrabbit evading a coyote's slashing jaws and jumped straight up into the air. The warrior's foot passed under him. Uncoiling both legs, Nate brought his soles crashing down on the Piegan's shin. The man let out a yelp, wrenched free, and staggered rearward.

Nate speared his knife out. It streaked beyond the eyedagg, the steel biting deep into the warrior's chest, but not deep enough to end their struggle. Springing out of reach, the Piegan grunted as scarlet drops sprayed from the jagged wound.

Among the trapping fraternity there was a common saying to the effect that a wounded bear was ten times more dangerous than usual. The same could be applied to humans. For now, venting a roar worthy of a grizzly, the warrior flailed the eyedagg without cease, seeking to batter the mountain man down by brute force.

Nate had to give ground or lose his life. His shirt was ripped, his leg suffered a hard bash, but so far he had saved himself from serious harm. A backhand swipe almost took him off guard. If he hadn't been holding the knife at chin level, his neck would have been ruptured from jaw to jugular.

The spike rang on cold steel. Nate was rocked onto his heels. Growling, the warrior pumped forward, the eyedagg sweeping lower. It was meant to tear into Nate's crotch but stroked between his legs instead. For a second the Piegan was off balance, overextended, unable to protect himself.

Their gazes met. Met and locked. The warrior's eyes mirrored the knowledge that he was going to die. He did not scream or howl. He did not go berserk in a futile paroxysm of defiance. Acceptance of the inevitable registered a fraction of an instant before the long knife sliced into his neck, cutting upward like a saber through butter.

Nate stood stock still except for his labored breathing. The Piegan was dead on his feet. The inner light faded, leaving a blank expression. Tugging the knife out, Nate stepped aside to avoid a scarlet torrent.

An unnerving silence claimed the prairie. Nate whirled, fearing the worst. Nearby sat Rufus Stern, dazed but otherwise unhurt. Over on the knoll was Isaiah Tompkins, hands on his knees, looking shocked to still be alive. Of McNair there was no sign.

"Shakespeare?" Nate bellowed, raw dread churning his innards. "Shakespeare?" He dashed to the slope and up it for a clear view, halting dead when the white-maned visage of his mentor appeared above the crest.

"What's all the hollering? A body would reckon you cared. I'm plumb flattered." McNair chortled. "More health and happiness betide my liege than can my care-tuned tongue deliver him.''

"The Piegans . . . ?''

Shakespeare gestured at two dead warriors at the north edge of the knoll and another on the south slope. To the east a lone horseman fled for his life. "That one valued his guts more than grit. The others gave as good as they got.''

Nate hunkered to wipe his knife clean on the grass. "The rest might show up before too long. We'd best head for the foothills while we still can.''

"Sage advice, I suppose, but I doubt the Piegans will plague us a second time. They've lost too many as it is. When they get back to their village there will be wailing and gnashing of teeth for days on end. Everyone will indirectly blame them.''

"And directly blame us. I wouldn't put it past them to have a war party pay us a visit in a few moons.''

"Maybe. Maybe not. I wouldn't lose any sleep fretting. Piegans generally don't venture too close to Ute country. And they'd have to get past the Shoshones first.'' Shakespeare shrugged. "What will be, will be, I always say.''

Isaiah Tompkins stared at his rifle in undisguised stupefaction. "I killed another human being,'' he marveled. "I took another's life.''

"Don't let it ulcerate your stomach,'' Shakespeare said. "If you hadn't, he'd have merrily dispatched you to the Hereafter and not missed a wink of sleep tonight. It was them or us, son. That's the short and sour of it.''

"Thou shalt not kill,'' Isaiah reminded him.

"Oh, that. Then what do you make of Ecclesiastes?'' Shakespeare envisioned the page in his mind's eye. "To every thing there is a season, and a time to every purpose under the heaven. A time to be born, and a time to die. A time to plant, and a time to pluck up that which is planted. A time to kill, and a time to heal.'' He paused. "Sort of contradicts the Commandment, don't you think?''

Isaiah had to ask, "How is it you can remember everything you've ever read?"

"It's a knack, is all. I was born with it."

"Remarkable."

Nate moved toward the other New Yorker, who had not budged. "Are you hurt?"

"No, I fell off the horse," Rufus confessed. The gelding had been spooked when King and the Piegan tangled, and he had been too weak to hold on. "I'm fine otherwise. Just so tired I could keel over."

"Don't fall asleep yet," Nate advised. Beyond Stern, to the northwest, roiling black clouds were billowing out over the prairie. "We're not quite out of the fire yet."

"What do you mean?"

The mountain man motioned. Rufus swiveled and saw vivid bolts of lightning lance the heavens.

"Ever seen a man charred to a crisp?" Nate King asked.

Chapter Four

Nature had gone mad. Half an hour later the raging tempest roared in upon them, and to Rufus Stern it seemed as if the Almighty had gone stark, raving berserk. He had seen storms before, but nothing to rival the terrifying fury of this one.

It began deceptively enough. First the wind picked up in gusts that grew in frequency and strength. In due course it shrieked and screamed like a raving harpy, buffeting them like an invisible battering ram.

Overhead, the sky darkened. Those great roiling clouds swallowed the sky, devouring it with remarkable rapidity. Never had Rufus beheld clouds like these. Gigantic beyond all measure, they billowed and heaved as if alive, as if they were living creatures endowed with all the ferocity Nature could conceive.

It was childish, Rufus knew, but he became scared. It brought back vague memories of his childhood, and how for a time he had been deathly afraid of thunderstorms. Many children were. And just like them, he had outgrown his fear. Or so he thought.

Now the fright returned, more potent than ever. Especially when Rufus saw flashes of elemental energy and heard the rumbling boom of distant thunder. Rumbling that came closer and closer as the flashes grew brighter and brighter. So many flashes, it gave the illusion someone had stockpiled kegs of block powder and was setting them off one after the other in a continuous chain.

The rain proved deceptive, too. Initially a few drops fell. Cold, hard drops that stung the skin. But the drops became larger as they descended in greater number. A steady rain fell for a while, a simple downpour. And just when Rufus believed that was as bad as it would get, the heavens opened, unleashing a titanic tempest the likes of which no human being would believe possible unless they experienced it themselves.

Rufus flinched and tucked his chin to his chest. It felt as if a thousand hard nails were poking his head and face, stinging unmercifully. He heard Isaiah curse. A glance at the mountain men showed them unaffected, sitting the big black stallion in impassive silence. They might as well be sculpted from granite for all the effect the storm had on them.

Suddenly, startling Rufus silly, horrendous bolts of crackling lightning and deafening crashes of thunder swept the prairie. The rain was a steady, solid wall of water, smashing against them in a wave. As weak as he was, Rufus feared being knocked off the gelding. So he clung to Isaiah and prayed to a God gone mad for deliverance.

But that was not the worst of it. Oh, no. Not at all.

The wind intensified. Howling as would a million wolves in raving chorus, it slammed into them as if seeking to bowl over their mounts. Rufus swore he could feel the white horse tense as it lowered its head and plunged on into the cataclysm.

By now the streaks of lightning rent the firmament without cease, one after the other after the other, some far off, but many very close, too close, so close Rufus saw them strike the ground, saw blasts of showery light and was rocked by thunder that threatened to shatter his eardrums. It dawned on him that a random bolt might well strike *them*. He remembered being told lightning usually hit the tallest objects in its vicinity. And on the flat plain, practically barren of trees or even high brush, *they* were the tallest objects to be found.

That was what Nate King had meant about being charred to a crisp. A lump formed in Rufus's throat, and he wished to hell he had never left New York City, wished to hell he had never let friendship impair his common sense. Sweet, wonderful Agnes had been right. He should have listened to her.

The next instant the sky was rent yet again. A bolt smashed into the earth not twenty feet away. Whinnying, the gelding veered. Rufus flinched, cowering as he had once cowered under his bed, his ears blistered, his nose tingling to an acrid odor. His hair tingled, too, some of it standing on end, and his skin was pricked all over as if by tiny pins. Isaiah cursed even more loudly. The mountain men, though, rode grimly on, unbent, uncowed, Nate King tall and straight in the saddle, Shakespeare McNair grinning up at the onslaught as if he were enjoying himself, a child at a fireworks display. The man truly was touched in the head.

How long they forged on, Rufus couldn't say. He only knew he was soaked and freezing and petrified and in abject misery. He only knew he wanted the storm to end. And he never wanted to experience another like it for as long as he lived.

Shakespeare McNair yelled something. Rufus looked, and saw the lunatic pointing to the northwest. Rufus gazed in that direction but saw nothing out of the ordinary. At first. How could he, with the sheet of rain and the pitch-black clouds? Then the rain slackened a little and the lightning revealed a sight that took his breath away.

The sky was alive. Part of it swirled around and around in the form of a giant funnel, the lower end whipping back and

51

forth like an airborne snake. A new sort of piercing howl climbed to a fever pitch. To Rufus's astonishment, the funnel ripped into a small isolated stand of trees, tearing them asunder like so much kindling. Trunks and limbs and leaves were sucked upward and flung every which way. "Sweet Jesus!" he said under his breath.

Shakespeare McNair shouted again. Rufus caught the word "twister." Then Nate King leaned out, grabbed the gelding's reins from Isaiah, and cut to the southwest, riding as if their very lives depended on it. And they did. For Rufus now saw that the twister, as McNair called the funnel, was bearing down on them like a steam engine gone amok, ripping out whole sections of sod. The funnel was expanding rapidly. Already it was forty to fifty yards wide and growing by ten yards every ten seconds.

"We're going to die!" Rufus yelled.

Isaiah Tompkins agreed. He had heard of tornadoes, but he had never thought he would see one. The thing mesmerized him. He clung to the saddle for dear life and watched it approach. It was so high, he had to tilt his head back to see the top. So powerful, it sheared into the earth itself. It was a Titan of old, one of the dawn creatures of antiquity, a living behemoth that would consume them whole. Isaiah didn't see why Nate King bothered to try to get away. There was no escape.

Nate King would have disagreed. As he was fond of saying, "Where there's life, there's hope." And so long as life remained, he would never go meekly to the other side. He would never give up. Especially not when he had a wife and children who loved him and depended on him. He would fight with all his might for the right to go on living for as long as the Good Lord allowed.

He didn't look at the tornado. He didn't have to. The ear-splitting roar it made told him exactly how close it was. And how close he was to meeting his Maker whether he wanted to or not.

Nate rode for all he was worth, goading the stallion to its limit and beyond. The gelding's reins were tight in his left hand, the white horse doing its best to hold to the same frantic pace. Both animals sensed impending doom. Both preferred to live. Although drenched and cold and tired, they put all they had into a herculean effort to fend off the seeming inevitable.

Shakespeare McNair stared at the twister, stared into its churning depths, and grinned. Fearsome as it was—and few things in life were more so—there was no denying the tornado was also magnificent. A thing of beauty. Perverse beauty, Nature at her worst, but beautiful nonetheless. He stared, and he marveled.

The leading edge was now sixty yards distant. Shakespeare could see grass being sucked out by the roots. Soon the funnel would do the same to them and they would be drawn up into its whirling heart. He wondered what that would be like, wondered whether they would live long enough to see what was inside.

Shakespeare remembered the time a twister had nearly killed Nate, the only man ever taken up by one and set down again later unharmed. Whenever he raised the subject, Nate clammed up. Would not talk about it, period. Which for Nate was downright strange. He was the most fearless person Shakespeare had ever known. So why wouldn't Nate say what it was like inside? Maybe, Shakespeare mused, Nate couldn't. Maybe there was no way to describe what it had been like in the belly of the beast.

More lightning illuminated the behemoth in all its brain-numbing glory. Shakespeare detected the churning silhouette of its southern side, nearly lost amid the background darkness. It would be a close shave. Very close.

Nate sensed the same. His every instinct shrieked to go faster, faster, but the stallion was already going as fast as it could go, faster than it had ever gone, faster then he had ever thought it could go. Pegasus was winded but keeping up. As for the two greenhorns, their faces were pale specters, their eyes as wide as saucers, the blood in their veins apparently frozen stiff. Rufus Stern's mouth worked as if he were going to scream, but to his credit the young New Yorker did not.

The tornado towered above them, a legendary maelstrom made real. The wind tugged at Nate, threatening to snatch him bodily and whirl him up and away as it had done once before, years ago. Many a night he had awakened in a cold sweat from harrowing dreams in which he relived the ordeal.

A miracle had spared him. What else could it have been? How else could anyone explain a man being snatched up into a whirlwind's inner core and living to tell the tale? And how could he ever describe that awful feeling of being suspended hundreds of feet in the air? That sickening sensation of swirling around and around and around until he was dizzy enough to wretch? Or the total, nerve-numbing, soul-wrenching horror of being completely and utterly helpless?

Nate hunched his shoulders against the twister's pull and slapped his legs against the black. The stallion's mane flew, its nostrils were flared.

Rufus Stern voiced a prayer. He was going to die, and he wanted to set himself right with God. He asked forgiveness for all the bad things he had done and apologized for not making more of his wretched life. From out of nowhere invisible fingers wrapped around his back and tried to pluck him loose, but he clasped Isaiah all the harder. "No! No! No!"

Shakespeare McNair laughed. Of all the ways he had envisioned meeting his end, this had not been one of them. What were the odds? He had no real regrets, other than not seeing Blue Water Woman again. Why should he, when he had lived a long, full life? Against the odds, he had lived to a ripe old age, outlasting by many years most of those who ventured to the Rockies decades ago when he did.

It had been a fine life, all told. Shakespeare had traveled more widely than any man alive. Young upstarts like Joseph

Walker and Jedediah Smith might one day surpass him, but he doubted it.

He had explored whole regions yet to be mapped. He had lived among tribes most whites had never heard of. He'd seen sights no one east of the Mississippi would believe. Huge geysers that spouted hissing steam. Pools of foul sulfur. Enormous clefts in the earth. A canyon so grand it was indescribable. And more creatures than he could shake a stick at. Bears that dwarfed Pegasus. Elk with racks that took two men to carry. Black mountain lions. Majestic eagles, devilish wolverines, white otters, and fish bigger than a buffalo. And then there were the hideous things, the creatures in the high lakes and those hairy two-legged giants who dwelled deep in ancient forests.

Yes, Shakespeare had lived a full life. He'd loved wonderful women, sired children. He had gorged on roasted buffalo, tasted fish eggs, eaten raw rattlesnake. He had laughed until he cried and cried until he laughed. He had done everything there was to do, and then some.

He had no complaints. But if he had his druthers, he would rather live on to savor more of life's rich harvest. For if there was one thing he had learned in his many years of existence, it was to live each day as if there would be no tomorrow. And above all, to be happy. Without happiness, nothing else counted for much. Without happiness, life was barely bearable.

A tug on his buckskin shirt snapped Shakespeare out of his reverie. The tornado was right on top of them. Another few moments and it would all be over. Then he saw the bottom of the funnel bounce upward, high overhead, and skip off to the north. Like the tapered end of a whip being flicked, it skipped hundreds of feet, alighted, and promptly bore to the northeast.

Shakespeare turned his face up into the pelting rain. "Not our time, huh?" he hollered. "Ay me, what act, that roars so loud and thunders in the index?"

The only answer was the yowling wind.

"There is a cliff whose high and bending head looks fearfully in the confined deep. Bring me but to the very brim of it, and I'll repair the misery thou dost bear with something rich about me. From that place I shall no leading need." Shakespeare chuckled gaily.

Nate heard his mentor speak, but the wind blasted the words into garble. He galloped madly on until McNair slapped him on the shoulder and leaned forward to be heard above the rain and the gusts.

"To be, Hamlet. That's the rub. To be." Shakespeare paused. "We're safe. It's gone, son, gone."

Nate had to see for himself. Even then he did not slow, not when lightning continued to pulverize the air and ground in a ceaseless bombardment. Unexpectedly, a broad gully yawned before them, a dark slash in the ground. He went down the slope without slowing. Reining up, he sprang off and held on to the bridle. "Hold Pegasus!" he shouted to Isaiah and Rufus.

Rufus was too dazed to do any such thing. He was numb from head to toe. Numb inwardly as well as outwardly. The merciless chilling rain had rendered his skin insensitive. The close call with the whirlwind had blunted his mind. Coherent thought eluded him.

Isaiah was wet to the bone. He was cold and hungry and stiff. But he was still in control of his faculties. So when the trapper yelled, he obeyed, sliding off and seizing the white mount's bridle and reins.

Rufus did not move. Mouth agape, he gawked heavenward. Rain deluged his tongue, seeping into his throat and making him sputter.

"Get down!" Shakespeare commanded. When the New Yorker did not do so quickly enough to suit him, he reached up and hauled Rufus off. Stern collapsed onto his hands and knees, quaking like a terror-stricken rabbit.

"Some folks never outgrow their diapers," Shakespeare commented, but it was lost in the gale.

A hint of gray to the west signified to Nate that they were about out of the woods. Presently the wind tapered, the rain slackened to a light shower. Lightning stopped rupturing the atmosphere, while the rumble of thunder drifted eastward.

Isaiah had been resting with his forehead pressed to Pegasus's neck. Rousing, he observed the aerial display dwindle. "It's over?" he breathed. "Really and truly over? We lived through it?"

"Unless we're dead and this is heaven," Shakespeare quipped. "I don't see any flames, so it can't be the other place."

"We survived!" Isaiah hiked his arms aloft. He started to titter, then tried to stop. But he could no more hold it back than he could stop the deluge. Hopping in exultation, he flapped his arms like an ungainly bird. "Oh, Lord! We survived!"

Shakespeare faced Nate. "Think how excited he would be if we had really been in danger."

Isaiah didn't care if the oldster poked fun at his expense. He was too supremely happy. So happy he danced a jig, laughing and clapping a hand against his rifle. "We did it! We did it!"

Shakespeare claimed Pegasus and loosened the saddle. "Do we move on?" he asked Nate. By his reckoning it was early yet, no later than nine or ten.

"Why bother? We're not going to find any place drier than here. And we're out of the wind."

Isaiah overheard. "You can't mean that. There's nothing to burn. How will we make a fire?"

"We won't."

"Then how will we dry out? Surely you can't intend for us to spend the whole night in wet clothes."

"They'll be mostly dry by morning," Nate predicted.

"But we'll catch our death."

Shakespeare had untied his parfleches and hunkered. Rummaging in one of the beaded pouches for some pemmican, he snickered. "Mister, after what we just went through, a few sniffles won't hurt you none."

Isaiah indicated Rufus, who had curled into a fetal position. "What about my friend? We can't leave him lying there on the ground. He's liable to come down with pneumonia."

"If he's that feeble, let him," Shakespeare said. Finding what he sought, he hungrily took a bite.

"That's harsh. Even for a man like you."

"*Life* is harsh, son. It doesn't have favorites. It never goes easy on anyone. Either we take what it throws at us and grow stronger, or we buckle and give in and give up the ghost. It's that simple."

"I hope to God I am never as callous as you are, sir."

"Callous, or honest?" Shakespeare bit off more. "Ay, sir. To be honest, as this world goes, is to be one man picked out of ten thousand."

Nate removed his saddle and blanket. Unfolding the latter, he gently draped it over Rufus Stern, who was sound asleep. "It's not much, but it should keep him warm."

Isaiah squatted, his rifle across his knees. What he wouldn't give for a crackling fire and a bowl of piping hot soup! Goose bumps covered him, his hair was plastered slick, and he had water in his right ear. Bending to the right, he smacked his head to force it out. "I swear. If I make it back to New York, I am never leaving again."

Curiosity impelled Shakespeare to ask, "What brought you to the wilderness, anyway? Did you think you'd be the next John Jacob Astor?"

"Not quite," Isaiah hedged. Everyone had heard of Astor, the richest man in America, thanks to wealth earned in the fur trade. Unbuttoning his shirt, he probed and latched on to his copy of *The Trapper's Guide*. The cover was soaked, some of the pages warped. "This is to blame." He tossed it to McNair.

"I should have known."

"You've seen it before?"

"Youngster, I've seen enough of these to pile to the moon. You're not the only poor fool to dream of making a lot of money without much effort."

Isaiah smiled. "Ahh. Then it is as easy as I thought it would be?"

It was Nate who responded. "Thomas, trapping is the hardest work you'll ever do. Let me tell you what a typical day is like."

"I already know," Isaiah crowed, tapping the manual. "A trapper gets up kind of early, fixes breakfast, then goes out to check his traps. He skins the beaver, carries their pelts back to camp, and sets them in a rack to dry. After a noonday rest—"

Shakespeare could not help himself. Cackling lustily, he clamped a hand over his mouth to stifle the noise.

Isaiah glared. "Is something wrong? I'll have you know this information comes on the best of authority. Sewell Newhouse, who wrote the manual, is the inventor of the Newhouse steel-jaw trap. It's used by trappers everywhere." Opening the *Guide* to a favorite page, he held it so the mountain men could see an artist's rendition of a stately trapper attired in a white shirt and dinner pants in front of a white tent. Beside the trapper a trusty dog was nobly poised. A canoe and a small mountain of neatly stacked supplies were prominent.

"Go on," Nate coaxed.

"Well, the *Guide* says that afternoons should be devoted to correspondence, cleaning guns if necessary, and whatnot. In the evening a leisurely supper is in order. After a good night's sleep, it's back to work the next morning." Closing the *Guide*, Isaiah replaced it under his shirt. "Not a bad life, if I do say so myself."

"Not at all," Shakespeare agreed, choking off more hilarity. "Makes me want to run up into the mountains and collect a ton of furs."

Isaiah fidgeted. "You're being sarcastic. All right. What is a trapper's day really like, then?"

Nate bent at the knees, balancing on the balls of his feet. "You wake up before first light and head out. There's no time for breakfast. You have to check the traps and get the beaver before they stiffen up on you. When you find one, you skin it on the spot, then move on to the next. It can take half the day. And most of that time you're up to your waist or higher in icy water. You're half frozen before the sun even rises."

"What's a little cold? That doesn't sound too awfully difficult," Isaiah said.

"Have you ever *seen* a real beaver?"

Isaiah coughed. "No, not really. But I've seen drawings of them. In here." He started to flip through the pages of the *Guide*.

Nate patiently explained, "A beaver can be up to four feet long and weigh upwards of sixty pounds. When it's wet, it is as slippery as an eel. And you have to reach down into that icy water, haul it high enough to open the trap, then lug it onto the bank so you can take off the hide. Sometimes your fingers are so cold, you can't hold the knife. When you're finally done, you reset the trap or move it to another spot. That means you have to go back into the water. By noon you're so stiff and cold you can hardly walk. Most trappers come down with rheumatism sooner or later."

"That's just the beginning," Shakespeare said, warming to the topic. "The hides have to be scraped clean. I like to smear the insides with the brains to keep them soft. And you can't forget to stretch them on a hoop for a couple of days. All that takes a lot of work."

Isaiah was beginning to appreciate exactly how exaggerated the *Guide* really was. "But you must have some time to yourself? Time to relax, to warm yourself at the fire? To write letters home?"

Shakespeare and Nate regarded each other. "No," both men

said simultaneously, and McNair resumed. "The horses need tending, traps must be cleaned and oiled. If you want to eat, you have to hunt. After a while, beaver meat gets mighty tiresome."

"You eat the beavers?"

"What else would you do, boy? Let all that meat go to waste?" Shakespeare shook his head. "Don't make that face. It's as tasty as can be. The tails are the best part. Charred, then boiled, they'll make your mouth water."

Somehow, Isaiah doubted it. "So you're saying there's never a spare moment?"

McNair nodded. "That's not all. If the cold water doesn't do you in, a sinkhole or an avalanche or a flood might. And you have to keep your eyes skinned for silvertips and Indians every second. I won't even mention the stomach complaints, or the fever." Shakespeare recalled the many men who had gone into the high country, never to return. "If you make it through your first year, you earn the right to be called a *hiverman*. Make it through three winters and you've done what not three men in a hundred have done."

"You give the impression trapping is next to impossible," Isaiah protested. "Fit for idiots and simpletons."

"That pretty much sums it up, yes."

"Then why are *you* a trapper? If it's everything you say, yet you keep at it, what does that make you?"

"The biggest damn idiot of all." Laughing, Shakespeare slapped his thigh.

Nate King was listening to the faint growl of thunder. "There's something else you should know, friend. When was that *Guide* of yours published?"

Isaiah had never thought to check. "Two years ago," he said after consulting the copyright. "Why? What difference does that make?"

"All the difference in the world." Nate would have gone on, but at that moment the growls acquired a new note.

Springing erect, he swung toward the east rim of the gully where a massive bulk loomed. He trained his Hawken on it but didn't shoot. "We have company," he announced.

"What?" Isaiah idly inquired. He had not looked up.

"A grizzly."

Chapter Five

At that instant a distant streak of lightning cast the bear in brief stark relief. Isaiah Tompkins saw the grizzly in profile, and the short hairs at the nape of his neck stood on end. It was enormous, seemingly as big as the bull buffalo. A trick of the light imbued its eyes with a spectral eerie glow. Tapered teeth flashed white, teeth as long as Isaiah's fingers, teeth capable of shattering bone with the same ease Isaiah would have biting into a soft piece of bread.

"Kill it!" Isaiah hollered. Leaping upright, he elevated his rifle.

Shakespeare McNair had been expecting some such foolishness. He was ready. Springing, he grabbed the barrel of the New Yorker's gun and snarled in Tompkins's ear, "Do that and we're all worm food! I've seen griz take eight to ten balls or better and not bat an eye. Just stand still and pray it's not hungry."

Stand still? Isaiah wanted to run, not stand there. Then he glanced at Rufus, sleeping soundly in blissful ignorance. The

63

beast would make short shrift of him. Isaiah gulped, quelled his fright, and prayed he was not making the biggest and last mistake of his life.

Nate King waited for the bear to make up its mind. That it had not attacked already was encouraging. But bears were so utterly unpredictable, it was impossible to predict what they would do next. This one might shuffle elsewhere or it might tear into them, huge paws churning.

Nate's main worry were the horses. Both stared hard at the grizzly, their ears pricked. Should either whinny or attempt to flee, it could set the bear off. Running from predators was a surefire invitation for trouble; it triggered a deeply ingrained instinct to chase and slay.

The silvertip moved a few feet along the rim with great, ponderous steps. Its bony slab of a head swung from side to side. Nate heard it sniff loudly, seeking to identify them by their scent.

An old mountaineer had once told him a grizzly was a "walkin' nose," and the frontiersman had hit the nail on the head. Grizzlies lived by their noses, drawn from one tantalizing scent to another. Whether rooting out rodents, ferreting a fawn hidden in high grass, or tracking down other prey, grizzlies relied mainly on their sense of smell.

Suddenly the lord of the wilderness reared onto its hind legs, rising and rising until it loomed a good eleven feet, large even by grizzly standards. The head craned upward as it continued to sniff.

Isaiah bit his lower lip to keep from yelling. He had a well-nigh irresistible impulse to shout at the creature to go away, to leave them alone, to find its supper elsewhere. His legs quivered, his stomach flipped and flopped.

Shakespeare was watching Pegasus. The gelding had a long-standing hatred for bears, ever since a grizzly tore open its flank when it was much younger. He wouldn't put it past Pegasus to go after the bruin.

GET
4 FREE BOOKS!

You can have the best Westerns delivered to your door for less than what you'd pay in a bookstore or online. Sign up for one of our book clubs today, and we'll send you **4 FREE* BOOKS**, worth $23.96, just for trying it out...**with no obligation to buy, ever!**

Authors include classic writers such as
LOUIS L'AMOUR, MAX BRAND, ZANE GREY
and more; PLUS new authors such as
COTTON SMITH, TIM CHAMPLIN, JOHNNY D. BOGGS
and others.

As a book club member you also receive the following special benefits:
- **30% OFF all orders through our website & telecenter!**
- **Exclusive access to special discounts!**
- **Convenient home delivery and 10 days to return any books you don't want to keep.**

There is no minimum number of books to buy,
and you may cancel membership at any time.
See back to sign up!

*Please include $2.00 for shipping and handling.

YES! ☐

Sign me up for the Leisure Western Book Club and send my FOUR FREE BOOKS! If I choose to stay in the club, I will pay only $13.44* each month, a savings of $10.52!

NAME: _____

ADDRESS: _____

_____

TELEPHONE: _____

E-MAIL: _____

☐ **I WANT TO PAY BY CREDIT CARD.**

☐ VISA   ☐ MasterCard   ☐ DISCOVER

ACCOUNT #: _____

EXPIRATION DATE: _____

SIGNATURE: _____

Send this card along with $2.00 shipping & handling to:

**Leisure Western Book Club
20 Academy Street
Norwalk, CT 06850-4032**

Or fax (must include credit card information!) to: 610.995.9274. You can also sign up online at www.dorchesterpub.com.

*Plus $2.00 for shipping. Offer open to residents of the U.S. and Canada only. Canadian residents please call 1.800.481.9191 for pricing information. If under 18, a parent or guardian must sign. Terms, prices and conditions subject to change. Subscription subject to acceptance. Dorchester Publishing reserves the right to reject any order or cancel any subscription.

JOIN NOW!

Nate pivoted, never taking his Hawken off the bear. One shot hardly ever brought a griz down. But he had slain enough of them to know where they were most vulnerable. Not the head, where a thick cranium rendered them virtually bullet proof. Nor the lungs, which were so large that it took several balls to prove fatal.

The best place to shoot a grizzly—the only place, in Nate's estimation—was in the heart. Their sheer bulk, though, made a heart shot difficult. The slug must pass through a couple of feet of solid sinew and various organs. And even when it hit home, such was the ferocious vitality of the brutes that they could live another couple of minutes before they succumbed. More than enough time to rip a man to literal shreds.

Nate braced himself when the bear stopped and looked at him. He could not see the eyes, but he could *feel* them bore into him. This was the moment of truth. The goliath was making up its mind. If it was going to do something, the next thirty seconds would tell.

Nate had no hankering to tangle with it, not after all the close shaves he'd had in previous years. Grizzly Killer, the Indian name bestowed on him, was fitting, for no one, no other trapper or Indian alive, had fought more of the monsters. At one time it had seemed to him that every time he turned around, another griz was there, jaws agape, slavering with ravenous hunger. As if he had been a magnet, drawing them to him from far and wide.

The bear halted. Nate fixed the barrel on where he believed the heart would be, but it was impossible to be sure in the inky darkness. He held his breath to steady his arm. Beside him, the stallion stirred, and he hoped to high heaven it wasn't about to do something that would ignite the bear's blood lust.

Then, grunting, the grizzly turned and lumbered off into the night, its huge pads going *splish-splish-splish* on the drenched ground. The sound soon faded.

Nate knew grizzlies were devious devils. They frequently

circled around to come at their prey from behind. But not this time. To the east the storm still raged, lightning still spewed from the heavens. Backlit against the faint glow was the bear's broad form, retreating off across the plain. "We're safe," he announced.

Shakespeare let go of the New Yorker's rifle and sank onto his haunches. The incident was forgotten before he stopped moving. As incidents went, it was another routine event in an adventurous life crammed with hair-raising escapades. As perils went, this one had been decidedly tame. To someone who'd had more hairsbreadth escapes than he had hairs on his chin, the bear's inquisitive examination did not rate a second thought.

Isaiah Tompkins, however, swore he would never forget it for as long as he lived. He had stared Death in its hairy face and lived. Should he make it safely back to New York, he would regale family and friends with the account. And perhaps no one would blame him if he embellished for dramatic effect.

Sitting, Isaiah held out both hands. They shook like leaves in a breeze. "Look at me!" he marveled. "Another minute of that and I don't know what I would have done."

Nate slid down to the stallion. "I reckon we've all had enough excitement for one day. Let's turn in. Dawn will be here before we know it."

"How can you sleep?" Isaiah responded. "I doubt I'll close my eyes all night."

Shakespeare curled onto his side. "Good. You can have first watch, then. Wake us if you hear anything. Or if the horses act like they do." Removing his beaver hat, he placed it under his head as a pillow. "Wake me in about three hours. Nate will spell me later."

Isaiah shook his head, astounded. He would never understand these mountain men if he lived to be a hundred. "How will I know when three hours is up? I don't have a watch."

Shakespeare surveyed the firmament. Scattered stars were

visible through breaks in the clouds. As luck would have it, one was the North Star. "See that star yonder?" he asked, pointing. When the younger man nodded, he moved his finger a couple of inches. "When it's about there, three hours will be up."

Isaiah watched Nate King stretch out on the cold, wet earth, cradle the Hawken, and close his eyes. How anyone could sleep under such trying conditions was beyond him. Isaiah certainly couldn't. His clothes were soaked, his body was chilled. He stood a very real risk of catching his death of cold.

Nearby, Rufus sawed logs. Isaiah envied him. Clasping his arms to his chest, he rubbed himself to try to warm up. He was hungry again, but he did not want to impose on the mountain men by asking for more pemmican. Between Rufus and him, over half of what the trappers had brought was gone.

The trappers. Isaiah studied them, the giant and the oldster. They were a peculiar breed, these mountain men. Evidently the tavern gossip was true. Tough as iron, fearless as panthers, able to live off the land, handy with a gun or knife, they were an independent bunch, as different from run-of-the mill folks as that grizzly had been from a common black bear.

Isaiah wondered what it was that turned ordinary men into mountaineers. Once upon a time Nate King was probably no different than Isaiah was. By what magic alchemy of circumstance and design had King been transformed? And why, once transformed, did so few mountain men return to the lives they had known? Why did King prefer the Rockies to New York City? What did he know that Isaiah did not?

A wavering howl pierced the gloom. Now that the storm had moved on, the prairie's nocturnal denizens were on the prowl again. Isaiah envisioned an army of red-eyed wolves slinking close to the gully and gripped his rifle firmly.

A yip to the south was answered by another to the northeast. Coyotes, Isaiah knew. A fluttering screech he could not identify. Most likely a doe or something else had fallen to a carnivore's slashing fangs and claws.

Isaiah could never get over how dangerous the wilderness was. A man never knew from one day to the next if he would be alive to greet the next dawn. Savages, wild animals, heat, cold, thirst, any one of them spelled doom if he wasn't careful.

Which added to the mystery of Nate King and McNair and others of their rugged ilk. What sane person would choose living in the wild over the comforts and culture places like New York City offered? Who in their right mind would pick survival of the fittest over a life of ease and pleasure?

Isaiah certainly wouldn't. He had learned his lesson. The hard way. City life was the only life for him. When he needed new clothes, all he had to do was visit his tailor. Not shoot a deer, skin it, treat the hide, cut it, then spend hours sewing it. When he needed food, all had to do was visit a tavern or the latest rage in fine eateries, a restaurant. Not kill something, butcher it, plop the meat in a pot, and wait for half an hour for the morsels to stew.

Isaiah had never truly appreciated how much a life of ease had going for it. Rather than spend most of his time attending to basic needs, in the city he had time to spare, time for the theater or concerts or socials. Time for women. Time for what mattered most in life.

Yet, in order to enjoy city life, a man needed money. Lots and lots of money. Which brought him back to what had brought him to the wilderness in the first place—namely, acquiring enough money to get a head start, enough to last him a good long while, enough to permit him to live in the lavish style to which he aspired.

Being a beaver trapper had seemed the ideal way. A year or two of easy, glamorous work and he would have had enough to launch him on the road to prosperity. But now the dream had been dashed on the cruel rocks of reality.

Or had it? Isaiah stared at the mountain men again. Maybe

he could persuade them to help. They must know every prime trapping site in the mountains. Places where the beaver were plentiful. If they could be persuaded to share a dozen traps, Rufus and he could salvage triumph from the dregs of disaster.

Deep in reflection, Isaiah did not think to check the star for a good long while. When he did, he was surprised to find it had gone past the spot indicated by McNair. Going over, he knelt and lightly placed a hand on the oldster's shoulder.

A knife flashed up and out and pressed against Isaiah's throat. Petrified, he gasped, "It's me! Tompkins! What are you doing?"

"By the Almighty," Shakespeare fumed. "Don't you know better than to wake a man like that? Give him a good swift kick, or smack him." Sliding the knife into its beaded sheath, he sat up.

"What did I do wrong?" Isaiah asked, gingerly rubbing his neck.

"Being so quiet. It's enough to make a coon think an Indian is about to lift his hair. Next time, make more noise so I'll know it's you."

Isaiah selected a flat spot and eased onto his back. Convinced he was too overwrought to rest, he pondered the strange quirks of fate that ruled a man's life. He did not realize his eyes had closed until he opened them and beheld a band of pink framing the horizon. A new day was dawning. "I'll be damned," he said aloud.

"So will nine-tenths of the human race." Shakespeare had been up for half an hour. He had wiped down Pegasus, thrown on his saddle, and was ready to depart.

Isaiah stiffly rose. His back felt as if he had spent six hours on a medieval torture rack. Rufus, incredibly, had not moved all night and was sound asleep yet. With a start, Isaiah discovered that the last member of their party was missing. "Where's King?"

"Checking on those ornery Piegans."

Nate had left an hour before. He had walked the stallion out of the gully so as not awaken the greenhorns, then swung up and trotted to the northeast. What with the storm and having lost half its members, the war party was unlikely to have gone very far.

Just so they don't come after us, Nate mused. Revenge was a dish best served steaming hot, and the Piegans were bound to be out for blood. "An eye for an eye" was a given west of the Mississippi. Turning the other cheek was unheard of—especially since to do so was considered cowardly.

Among the Shoshones a man always avenged the slaying of a loved one. If, say, the Pawnees raided a Shoshone village, a prominent warrior was bound to propose paying the Pawnees a visit to retaliate. Then the Pawnees would need their revenge. And so on and so on. A vicious cycle, with no one the clear winner and everyone poorer for the loss of life and property.

There were exceptions, as there were to every rule. The Cheyennes and the Arapahos had become the best of friends. The Shoshones and the Flatheads were on amicable terms after many years of strife. And even the dreaded Lakotas had recently agreed to a truce with their longtime enemies, the Crows.

But the exceptions were few. By and large, Indians were their own worst enemy. The red race had been at war with itself for so long, whole tribes were devoted to the pursuit of war to the exclusion of all else. Each boasted several warrior societies. Men sought to outdo one another by counting the highest number of coup. For with coup came prestige, respect, influence. With coup came the prettiest women, the biggest lodges, the most horses.

Indian men who wanted no part of warfare were treated as women. They were made to do the work women did, made to perform endless drudgery, made to associate with the women all day, every day. Made to look like complete and total asses. A few short moons of this treatment and practically any man was ready to take up his bow and lance, paint his face, and go off to kill.

Nate occasionally liked to ponder how different history would be if Indians had learned to band together against common foes. It was doubtful, for instance, that the early French and English forces could have taken over so much land so swiftly if the Iroquois and the Hurons had been allies instead of bitter enemies whose hatred was so cleverly exploited.

To the north several large animals grazed. Nate absently looked at them, turned away, then looked again. They were horses. Indian warhorses, paint and all. He was willing to wager they belonged to the Piegans. But what were they doing by themselves? Had they broken loose during the storm? He veered to catch two for the New Yorkers to use, but the war mounts sped off with tails high.

Rather than tire the stallion so early in the day, Nate let them go. Farther on he spotted another four to the southeast. For a few to stray was within the bounds of reason. For most to have done so was unthinkable. The Piegans would never let that happen.

Nate had a hunch where he would find their camp. When the knoll came into view, he slowed and circled. On the other side lay the war party's camp. The Piegans were still there, scattered willy-nilly, some near the knoll, others out in the grass. Dark splotches dotted many of the prone figures. Some were rimmed by reddish pools.

Nate kept circling until he found clear prints heading to the east. Enormous tracks, fourteen inches from the heel to the tips of the middle claws. So fresh that Nate rose in the stirrups and was rewarded with a glimpse of the grizzly in the distance.

Dismounting, Nate led the stallion into the camp—or what was left of the camp. Shredded blankets, busted bows, and broken lances were scattered all over. Bodies were everywhere. One Piegan had been torn open from sternum to crotch. Another had half a face. Still another had been rent limb from limb, the torso cut to ribbons. But the man's head had not been touched and his features were set in quiet repose.

Nate had to avoid scores of body parts. Legs, arms, chunks of stomachs and chests, even entire heads. Several Piegans had been partially eaten.

As best Nate could reconstruct what occurred, it went like this. The war party had made camp at the base of the knoll. Shortly afterward, the storm had struck and the Piegans had huddled against its onslaught. When the tempest subsided, they'd lain down to sleep.

The grizzly had come on them in the middle of the night. It was among them before they knew it was there, ripping and rending, dispatching a third or more as they lurched erect, sleepy-eyed and dull-witted.

A slaughter had taken place. Bows and arrows and knives were useless against a living mountain. The bear had mowed the Piegans down as a scythe mowed grain. They fought valiantly, running close to sink their shafts, but in the end the bear's stamina was too much for them. It slew every one.

At the end a few wounded warriors had tried to escape, but the grizzly chased each down. To the bear it must have been grand sport. Like snatching fish one after the other from a river. Only in this case it had been ripping Piegans into oblivion.

There were too many to bury even if Nate were of a mind to, which he wasn't. They were his enemies. They had tried to ambush him. Their grisly fate was richly deserved.

He salvaged what he could. A steel knife with a bone handle. A parfleche decorated with elaborate beadwork. A rawhide rope. A few other things. He was making a last sweep when the stallion nickered.

Several hundred yards out, the grizzly loped toward them. In a lithe bound Nate gained the saddle, wheeled the big black, and fled up and over the knoll. Why it had come back he would never know. For a quarter of a mile he held the stallion to a gallop, relenting only when the bear gave up. Rising onto its hind legs, it stayed erect until he was out of sight.

By then the sun had risen. They would get a late start. Nate pushed on until he spied the same four horses to the south. They were resting. Procuring the rawhide rope, he fashioned a noose. The quartet observed his approach anxiously. When he was close enough to chuck a stone and hit them, a dusky warhorse snorted and raced away. The others followed suit.

Nate slapped his heels against the stallion. Rather than try to catch the swiftest, he picked the slowest, a tan animal on which a vivid red hand had been painted. The noose at his side, he rapidly overtook it. Sluggish from lack of sleep and having grazed until it was fit to burst, the warhorse was no match for the big black. It slowed to a walk within half a mile.

Wary of being bitten, Nate rode in as close as he dared and flicked the noose. The Piegan animal ducked, skipped to the left, and was off again like a shot. But Nate kept pace, coiling the rope for another try. The next time the warhorse slowed, the rope licked out and slipped over its head.

Expecting resistance, Nate turned the stallion broadside and hauled on the rawhide. But the warhorse stopped and stood docile, as meek as a lamb. Like a dog on a leash, it didn't act up when he headed for the gully.

The questioning screech of a hawk drew Nate's attention to a pair soaring high overhead. A high-pitched squeal alerted him to a prairie dog colony, which he wisely avoided. Bees buzzed by in search of nectar. Small birds flitted among colorful flowers.

Nate inhaled the fragrant morning air, relishing the moment. Life thrived on the prairie and in the mountains. Raw life. Often savage life, often harsh. Yet life that radiated zest and vitality, life the likes of which most city dwellers never experienced.

The wilderness possessed a special quality, an elusive quality that imbued those who had the grit to live in the wild with a keen relish for living. With the same zest and zeal exhibited by life itself.

Nate would never go back. Not if someone were to offer him a million dollars. Once an uncle had done something similar. Had offered him a substantial sum if only he would forsake Winona and return to civilization, "where he belonged."

It went without saying that Nate declined. He hadn't bothered to explain why. For it was impossible for those who had tasted the delicious fruit of pure freedom to describe the sterling taste to those who were used to the dull, drab table scraps society claimed made a person free.

A lot had changed since Nate left. From newcomers he learned about the state of the Union, how each year cities grew more and more crowded, how each year Congress passed more and more laws, how each year the precious freedom Americans secured during the Revolution was being chipped away bit by bit. Nate doubted whether the average citizen a few short generations hence would know what true freedom truly was.

What had Scott Kendall once told him? The feisty trapper had once wintered in Nate's valley, and in the evenings they had sat around the fire jawing about books and politics and religion. All those things trappers were supposed to be too dumb to understand.

Once, Scott had mentioned a quote from Epictetus, a quote that stuck in Nate's skull ever since. "No man is free who is not master of himself." Truer words had never been written.

Nate took stock of the multitude of life flourishing on the plain, and beamed. All those creatures—as free as the wind. Humankind could be equally free if only it would shake off the shackles imposed by those who thought they had the right to impose their ideas of how everyone should live whether everyone wanted to live that way or not.

Suddenly a shadow passed in front of him. Snapping erect, Nate raised the Hawken. It was only a raven, the rhythmic beat of its wings as clear as crystal.

Breaking into a trot, the mountain man presently saw a white-maned figure materialize as if out of nowhere and wave.

"Here comes Hamlet," Shakespeare said for the benefit of the New Yorkers. Rufus Stern was finally up and stuffing himself with pemmican. Isaiah, oddly quiet since Nate left, at the moment was cleaning his rifle.

"About time," the latter declared. "Half the morning is gone."

"In a hurry, are you?"

Isaiah paused in the act of shoving a patch of cloth down the barrel with his ramrod. "Yes, I am. Which reminds me. How soon before we reach the damn Rockies? I am so sick of grass, I could vomit."

"Do tell. You're in luck, then, hoss."

"In what respect?"

"Those mountains you have such a powerful hankering to see are a lot closer than you reckon."

Something in the frontiersman's tone brought Isaiah to his feet. He had not left the gully since they arrived the night before, and his legs were wooden as he awkwardly climbed to the west rim. Intent on not losing his footing, he did not lift his head until he was at the top. The sight that met his gaze jolted him.

"God in heaven! Where did *they* come from?"

Chapter Six

Shakespeare McNair chuckled. "They weren't there yesterday. Do you suppose they sprouted overnight like that beanstalk did?"

Isaiah Tompkins didn't hear. He was in shock, riveted to the vista spread out before his wondering gaze.

The mountain man had seen the same reaction before. Most who set eyes on the majestic Rockies for the first time were overwhelmed. And who could blame them?

As it turned out, the gully was located some five hundred yards from the leading edge of emerald foothills high enough to qualify as mountains east of the Mississippi. But here the foothills were no more than footstools, very small footstools, compared to the titans they fringed.

Magnificent. It was the one word that came anywhere close to describing the Rocky Mountains in all their supreme glory. And even that didn't do them complete justice. The Rockies had to be seen to be fully appreciated.

Rising thousands of feet above sea level, they formed a

gigantic wall stretching from Canada almost clear down to Mexico. Over three thousand miles, some claimed. Near the center of the chain, where Nate had his homestead, reared some of the highest. One was Long's Peak, a spectacular summit crowned practically year-round by a mantle of pristine snow. Not quite three miles high, it was breathtaking to behold, especially for first-timers like Tompkins and Stern.

Shakespeare chortled when Rufus joined his friend and the pair surveyed the spectacle in dumbfounded silence. It had taken his breath away, too, lo, those many years ago when he first crossed the plains. Somehow he had known on that very day he would never go home again, never again taste the tainted fruits of civilization. Those glittering gigantic spikes thrusting skyward held an allure impossible to resist.

He had no regrets about his decision. In all the years he had lived in the wild, it was safe to say he'd never had a dull moment. Each and every day was a sparkling new adventure unto itself, which would not have been the case had he gone home. Maybe he'd have farmed, or tried his hand at being a blacksmith, or at running a mercantile. Decent enough work, but it paled against the luster of the untamed wilderness.

A nicker from the black stallion heralded Nate's arrival. He descended into the gully and rode up the other side. The astonishment etching the faces of the greenhorns amused him. "Didn't Newhouse mention the Rockies in that *Guide* you're so fond of?"

Isaiah numbly nodded. "No words can do them justice, though. They're beyond belief."

"They're beautiful," Rufus said. Which struck him as funny. He had never thought things could be beautiful, only people. Yet the fantastic array of rugged peaks, some glistening white as ivory, were as lovely as his beloved Agnes.

"Got a present for you," Nate said, tossing the reins to the Piegan horse at Tompkins. "You'll have to ride double. But we'll make a lot better time with three animals."

Isaiah tore his eyes from the Rockies. "Isn't this an Indian's? Where did you get it?"

"From a Piegan who has no further use for it." Nate stretched to relieve a kink in his lower back, then glanced at his mentor. "Are you planning on wasting the day away? Or can we light a shuck?"

"Thither shall it, then. And happily may your sweet self put on the lineal state and glory of the land!" Shakespeare answered.

Rufus blinked. "What did he just say?"

"He can't wait to get back and cram his mouth with food until he bursts," Nate joked.

Shakespeare feigned indignance. "I said no such thing, Hamlet, my prince, and you damn well know it." Placing a hand to his forehead as if he were in torment, he quoted, "Why, look you, I am whipped and scourged with rods, nettled and stung with pismires."

"Huh?" Rufus said.

Nate bent down. "Want some free advice, friend? Ignore him if you want to keep your sanity." He glanced at McNair. "As for you . . ." It took a few seconds for him to remember the right quote. "I know thee not, old man. Fall to thy prayers. How ill white hairs become a fool and a jester."

Cackling lustily, Shakespeare slapped his thigh. "I'll be! You *have* been paying attention all these years! And here I figured all my recitals went in one ear and out the other." Tremendously pleased, he swung onto Pegasus. "Tell you what. With a little coaxing, I could be persuaded to read *Julius Ceasar* as we go along."

"No, thanks," Nate said. Once McNair started reading from old William S., there was no stopping him.

"Very well, then. With no coaxing at all." Fishing in a parfleche, Shakespeare produced his well-worn copy of *The Complete Works of Shakespeare*. The cover was battered, many of the pages dog-eared, but otherwise it was in fine condition. His wife liked to joke that he took better care of the book than he did of her.

Opening it to the correct page, Shakespeare cleared his throat. "Act One, Scene One. Rome. A street. Enter Flavius, Marullus and certain Commoners. Flavius speaks—"

Rufus turned to the younger mountain man. "He's not really going to read the whole play, is he? Not the *whole* thing?"

"I hope you brought wax to plug your ears with." Nate prodded the stallion into motion. "It's going to be a long ride."

Isaiah and Rufus hastily mounted. They did not know what to say when McNair brought Pegasus alongside their mount.

"Are you ready for a real treat?"

"If you say so," Isaiah responded. He'd been to a Shakespearean play once and hated every minute. Boring did not begin to describe the flowery language and the silly antics of the actors.

"Hence!" Shakespeare began, gesturing grandly and booming loud enough to be heard in St. Louis. "Home, you idle creatures, get you home. Is this a holiday? What! Know you not—"

Rufus put his mouth to Isaiah's ear. "King is right. This *is* going to be a long ride."

"Maybe not. Maybe he'll get so carried away, he'll fall off his horse and break his neck."

"We should be so lucky."

They weren't. Over the next several hours the New Yorkers were treated to recitals of *Julius Ceasar, Measure For Measure,* and *Pericles.*

"So, on your patience evermore attending," Shakespeare concluded, "New joy wait on you! Here our play has ending."

"Thank God," Isaiah muttered.

Shakespeare closed the big book with a crisp snap. "What was that, hoss? Didn't catch it?"

"I said thanks for entertaining us."

David Thompson

"Think nothing of it. Tonight I'll read *King Henry VI,* Parts One, Two, and Three. And if there's time, I'll throw in *Titus Andronicus* for good measure."

"Good God."

"I know, I know. Sounds too good to be true. At the rendezvous there are usually twenty to thirty coons gathered around each night just to hear me. I reckon you could say I've become a legend in my own time." Shakespeare snickered while sliding the volume back into the parfleche.

"You're something, that's for sure," Isaiah conceded. "But what was that you just mentioned? The rendezvous?"

"The annual get-together for the trapping fraternity. Free or company men, it doesn't matter. Takes place each summer. Mostly up on the Green River." Shakespeare paused. "Or rather, it used to take place. Word is that this year's will be the last."

"How's that?"

McNair sighed. "It's what Nate started to tell you yesterday when he asked how long you'd owned Newhouse's manual. All that business about trappers earning a lot of money. It's no longer true."

A new kind of fear speared through Isaiah. "What are you dithering about? Beaver hats are still popular. So are capes and cloaks with beaver trim."

"Not as popular as they used to be," Shakespeare said. "The market for peltries bottomed out a couple of years ago and never recovered. Once, the fur companies were offering up to nine dollars a hide. Now you're lucky if you can sell prime pelts for three or four."

Isaiah was not to be deterred. "That's still a lot—"

"Think so? Not when black powder costs close to three dollars a pound, and a new blanket will set you back fifteen." Shakespeare ran a hand through his beard. "I'm right sorry to be the bearer of bad tidings, boys, but you've set your compass by a star that just ain't there. The trapping business has gone

80

to hell. With only one rendezvous left, you'd be lucky to break even.''

Dismay ate at Rufus like an acid. "Please. There has to be a way. There just has to be. We've come so far. Been through so much. And we invested over two hundred dollars of our own money to buy the supplies and horses we lost.''

Isaiah was thinking of the ridicule that would be heaped on their heads if they went back to New York as failures. Everyone would say, "We told you so!" They would never hear the end of it. "There must be a way,'' he echoed.

Shakespeare felt sorry for the pair. As greenhorns went, they weren't too obnoxious. Just misguided. A common enough shortcoming. He would like to help, but he couldn't imagine how. The small nest egg he had socked away wouldn't do them much good. "I can't think of one." he admitted.

Crestfallen, Isaiah lowered his chin to his chest. So much for his vaunted dream! So much for buying a house of his very own! He could forget the small country estate that had taken his fancy. He could forget the fine carriage he wanted, and courting the daughters of wealthy men so he could marry into even more money.

"What will Agnes say?" Rufus wondered aloud. Would she laugh at him? Call him dull-witted, as others sometimes did? No, not sweet Agnes. She would hug him and tell him to listen to her advice next time. And he would. From then on, whatever she wanted, he would do. Wasn't that what made the perfect husband?

Nate King heard the exchange but offered no comment. The New Yorkers had made a mistake. They must live with the consequences. At least they were alive, which was more than could be said about three-fourths of those who braved the wilds to obtain a poke of jingling coins.

Isaiah wanted to throw back his head and scream in impotent fury. Once again life had treated him unfairly. Once again the Fates had flung his hopes and aspirations back into his face. Distraught, he glanced up. They were high in the foothills by now, following a narrow winding trail he could never have found on his own. The vegetation consisted mostly of pines and scrub brush. Mountains towered above, reaching to the clouds.

Ahead, Nate King rounded a bend onto a wide shelf, his head bent as he inspected his Hawken. McNair was staring to the south. Only Isaiah saw the lone rider waiting on the shelf. He saw beaded buckskins, a bow and quiver, long black hair worn in a loose mane, and a dark, angular visage. "Nate, look out!" he bawled. "A savage!"

Isaiah drew rein and started to lift his rifle. He thought he was fast, but the figure was liquid quicksilver. The bow elevated, the string was pulled smoothly back, and a barbed tip was lined up with Isaiah's chest, all in the bat of an eyelash.

"No!" Nate hollered, cutting the stallion so he was between the greenhorn and the horseman. "Lower your weapons, the both of you!"

Isaiah was incredulous. The mountain man had put himself in the arrow's line of flight and was bound to take the shaft in the side. The Indian had the string next to his cheek, below the eye. "In heaven's name, get out of the way!"

Nate gestured. "I meant it! Keep that rifle down." To the savage Nate said, "What are you waiting for? Winter to set in?"

"Ahhhh, Pa. He was fixing to shoot me. What else was I to do?"

Had Isaiah heard correctly? The Indian just called King "*Pa*"?

"This man is our guest, Zach. He's to be treated with the same hospitality you'd show Touch the Clouds or Drags the Rope." Nate kneed the stallion over next to his son's roan and placed his hand on the boy's shoulder. "Don't fault him if he's a mite wolfish. We tangled with some Piegans yesterday. Barely got away."

Zachary King lowered his ash bow while rising on his horse to see past the pair of silly whites in their grungy store-bought clothes. "Are they still after you?" he asked eagerly. "Want me to slow them down?"

Nate King smiled, but a small shadow clouded his heart. His son had grown into a strapping young man. Barely seventeen, Zach appeared to be two to three years older. The boy had Nate's broad shoulders and square chin, his powerful frame and supple grace. But Zach still had a lot of growing up to do inside, where it counted most. "No need. A grizzly rubbed the whole bunch out."

"Oh." Zach made no attempt to hide his disappointment. "I was hoping to count some coup. Piegan scalps are as good as any other."

Nate's smile evaporated. Sometimes he found it hard to accept that this was the same carefree boy Winona and he had raised, the same innocent soul who once refused to kill a spider because he couldn't bear to hurt a living thing. Now all his son cared about was earning glory in battle. "Piegans are people, just like us."

"What's that mean?" Zach responded.

"If I need to explain, you wouldn't understand." Nate clapped his son's back, then moved on, toward the high defile that would take them to the secluded valley he had claimed as his own.

Confused, Zach focused on the one man whose insights he valued as highly as his father's. "What did I say, Uncle Shakespeare?"

"He's probably tired, is all, Stalking Coyote," McNair hedged, using the boy's Shoshone name. "Think of it no more. For nature crescent does not grow alone in thews and bulk. But, as this temple waxes, the inward serve of the mind and soul grows wide withal."

"That's nice, but he's upset with me and I'd like to know why." Zach turned the roan to catch up with his father, pausing long enough to scrutinize the greenhorns. They were typical whites, he suspected—unwashed, ignorant of the ways of the wilderness, and headstrong. "Nice hair," he told the one who had tried to shoot him.

"Thanks," Isaiah replied, perplexed by the peculiar compliment. Up close he could see how young the son really was. A combination of traits, both white and Indian, branded him a half-breed.

"I bet it would look great hanging from a peg in our cabin." Laughing, Zach hurried his horse along, yelling, "Pa! Pa! Wait up."

Isaiah felt a flush of resentment. "What's the matter with that boy? Why did he treat me so rudely?"

"He's at that age," Shakespeare said.

"What age?"

"Where he thinks he knows all there is to know. And, for a Shoshone, where coup means everything. He's already counted enough to rank as a warrior, but he's not satisfied. One day he aims to be a leader, a war chief maybe."

Rufus perked up. "Good heavens. Are you saying that child has killed people? And scalped them?"

Shakespeare wagged a finger. "I wouldn't go calling him a child to his face, were I you. You saw how adept he is with a bow? Well, with a knife he's a regular hellion." Shakespeare resumed riding. "Besides, he's not all that younger than either of you. Four or five years would be my guess. Out here that practically makes him a grown-up."

Rufus could not get over the idea of the son of a white man lifting scalps. "I don't care how old he is. How can he cut off someone else's hair? It's inhuman. Indecent."

"He must take after his mother, not his father," Isaiah opined.

Shakespeare's head snapped around so abruptly, he nearly lost his hat. "Let me give you another word of advice, pilgrim. If you ever insult Nate's wife like that in his presence, you'll find out the father and the son have a lot more in common than you think.''

Twenty yards up the trail, Zachary King overtook his father. ''Ma sent me, Pa. She was worried when you didn't show up last night like you should have.''

''She sent you? Or you pestered her to come look for us so you could get away on your own for a spell?''

Zach grinned. ''A little of both, I guess. But I did ask Drags the Rope and Touch the Clouds to go with me. They couldn't be bothered. Tomorrow they leave, and they were busy helping their wives pack.'' He fluttered his lips. ''It ain't right. Great warriors like them doing women's work.''

''Don't criticize what you don't understand. Once you have a wife of your own, then you can talk.'' Nate softened his voice. ''I do my share of work around our cabin, don't I? And no one has ever accused me of being puny.''

Zach had to admit his father had a point. His pa was widely regarded as a fearless foe, as someone to be reckoned with. The Shoshones, the Crows, the Flatheads, the Cheyennes, even the Utes held him in high regard. Zach felt no small amount of pride at being the mighty Grizzly Killer's son.

Yet, strangely enough, his pa also liked to help his ma around the cabin. Cleaning, doing dishes, even folding clothes, his father was not above lending a hand. It mystified Zach no end. A warrior should never stoop to do menial work.

Zach would do none of that stuff when *he* was married. Warriors should devote themselves to war. To practicing with various weapons for hours on end. To fashioning arrows and bows, to cleaning guns, to sharpening knives, to taking care of prized warhorses. Those kinds of things.

''We'll have to go hunting at first light,'' Nate mentioned. The family's larder was lower than normal. He had gone to the prairie after fresh buffalo meat, but now they must make do with an elk or a deer. In another week or so he would go again, after the greenhorns had been sent on their way.

"What happened to the packhorse you left with?" Zach inquired.

"Painter got it our first night out."

"Darn. I liked that critter. Hardly ever bit me. It's not as mean as that piebald we got from the Crows. Never can trust those pesky coyotes to deal fair and square." Zach brightened at an inspiration. "I know. Instead of going hunting, why don't we butcher the piebald and eat it?"

Nate looked at his son. The notions he came up with! "We wouldn't eat horse meat unless we were starving."

"Why not? Spotted Bull told me the Apaches eat horse meat. And everyone says the Apaches are the best fighters alive."

Nate did not need to be reminded. Years ago, when Zach was half the age he was now, the family had ventured to Santa Fe, more as a lark than anything else. Shakespeare and Blue Water Woman had tagged along, and the trip had gone well until they reached the Mexican province of New Mexico.

There, one night, Apaches raided a *rancho* they were staying at. Winona had been kidnapped. Nate had set out in pursuit, and after an ordeal worthy of Daniel Boone he again held her in his arms. But it had been close; he'd nearly lost her forever.

So Nate had all the firsthand experience with the dreaded and deadly Apaches he wanted, thank you. And if he never went up against them again, it would be none too soon.

"Spotted Bull says the Apaches are tougher than the Comanches and the Blackfeet combined," Zach divulged. The former were the scourge of the southern plains, while the Blackfeet had long held sway over the northern sections.

"They might just be," Nate said. "But remember what I told you about being tough. There's always someone somewhere a little tougher. One day the Apaches will meet their match."

Zach could not conceive of such an event, but if his pa said it, it must be true. "How long will those greenhorns be staying with us? More than a couple of days?"

"Probably. Why?" Another disturbing issue for Nate was his son's thinly disguised contempt for most whites. A recent development, neither Nate nor Winona could explain it. "They were lost. Indians stole their horses and their provisions."

"Right out from under their noses, I'll bet." Zach laughed. In the wild most whites were as helpless as newborn babes. His father and Uncle Shakespeare and a few others were truly at home, but even most seasoned trappers couldn't hold a candle to the Shoshones. And it was his mother's people Zach admired more than any other.

Each year since his birth the family had spent the summer months among them. His first riding lesson had been courtesy of Spotted Bull, his mother's uncle. His first archery lesson had been given by Drags the Rope, whose skill with a bow was renowned in the tribe.

Each year Zach had been drawn more and more to the Shoshone way of living, and less and less toward the beliefs of his father's people. He never came right out and said so for fear of hurting his father's feelings.

"Don't be so hard on them, Stalking Coyote," Nate advised. "In a big city you would be just as helpless as they are here."

"I doubt that," Zach declared. He had every confidence in his ability to survive any situation. Hadn't he bested bears, cougars, and Blackfeet? "From what you've told me, a city has everything a person needs. Food, clothes, weapons. And I speak the white tongue fluently."

"There's more to surviving among white men than knowing English or where to find a hot meal." Nate did not go into detail. One day—soon, possibly—he intended to take his loved ones east to a city. Perhaps St. Louis. So the children could experience the white man's world for themselves and see that, overall, it had more good elements than bad.

The irony wasn't lost on him. He wanted nothing to do with civilization, he had forsaken his heritage to live in the wilderness, yet it upset him when his flesh and blood showed disdain for the very things *he* disliked.

Zach was talking. "... had that same cat pay us a visit. Leastwise, we think it was the same one. It came down close to the cabin last night and made a ruckus. Screeching and growling something awful. The horses nearly broke out of the corral."

Nate's lips compressed. A mountain lion had plagued their valley since early spring, defying all his attempts to trap or shoot it.

"Touch the Clouds and Drags the Rope went after it, but the painter vanished like a ghost, just like it always does."

"Sooner or later it will make a mistake," Nate predicted. In that respect animals were similar to humans. No matter how savvy they were, eventually they were careless, and in the mountains being careless usually carried a fatal price.

The trail steepened. On either side rose unscalable rock cliffs. Funneled steadily higher toward a gap at the summit, Nate roved the ground for sign of game. Deer and elk tracks were abundant. A black bear had passed by within the past day. And he saw more chipmunks than he could shake a stick at.

The air grew cooler. They negotiated a switchback, coming out on a rounded barren spur. Nate was halfway across when a clear set of tracks in soft dirt caught his eye. Reining up, he noted their size and depth.

Zach whistled, then chuckled. "This cat's a big one, sure enough. Any bigger and I'd swear it must be part grizzly."

Nate was not amused. Not one little bit.

"Do you reckon it followed you down and killed your packhorse?"

Nate had never even considered that. But the tracks did

point toward the prairie, and they had been made three days before. A chill swept through him, a chill not caused by the high altitude. So far the painter had killed two of his horses. Next it might be one of his family.

Chapter Seven

Winona King considered herself fortunate.

She was the mate of a man who was everything she had ever hoped to find in a husband. A man she loved as passionately now as she had during the heady rush when they courted—as whites would say. They had a fine lodge, or cabin, and were situated in a pristine valley close to an azure lake. Game was abundant, so they never lacked for food. Two fine children lent luster to their marriage.

As far as belongings went, she was much better off than many of her Shoshone sisters. Plenty of clothes, many fine cooking utensils, enough blankets to last a lifetime all were hers. Nine horses were another example of the riches she enjoyed. Or eight, rather, since one had been devoured by a cat. Yes, when Winona thought about her status in life, as she was doing this sunny day while on her way to the lake to fetch a bucket of water, she rated herself extremely fortunate.

She was no misty-eyed dreamer, though. She would be the first to admit her husband had a few flaws. Some, such as being as stubborn as a bull buffalo, and much too protective, were traits common to all males. Men could not help being men. Red or white, it made no difference. They loved to puff themselves up like grouse and strut in front of their women. They thumped their chests and boasted of battles won, glories gained. They always had to have the fastest horse, the best gun, strongest bow, or longest lance.

Even Nate was susceptible. He never formally counted coup as Shoshone warriors did, yet secretly he took pride in having counted more than most. And his accomplishments as a hunter and grizzly fighter had spread the name of Grizzly Killer far and wide.

In fact, Winona was more proud of his reputation than he was. Among her people the bravest men were always held in the highest esteem. And her husband had proven his courage time and again by facing the mightiest beasts in all the wilderness and besting them in vicious claw-against-steel combat.

So now, as she came to the lakeshore and paused to revel in the marvelous beauty of the tranquil scene, Winona smiled and said softly, "I am truly happy."

The setting alone was enough to induce good cheer. The lake shimmered blue in the bright sunlight, while above her white fluffy clouds sailed tranquilly along. Ducks paddled merrily, geese sailed majestically. Regal peaks reached to the ether, a ring of mountains that sheltered the valley on all sides.

It was a special place, imbued with good medicine. Her intuition had told her so the first time she set foot there. A sense of peace had permeated her being. Peace and belonging. As if she had come home to a home she had never known but somehow knew. Though that made no rational sense.

Bending to dip the bucket into the water, Winona saw her reflection. Her waist-length raven hair, her oval face, the features Nate swore were the loveliest of any woman who ever lived. The red lips he loved to kiss. The smooth brow he loved to stroke.

She froze on seeing tracks in the soft mud at the water's edge. Not human tracks. *Cat* tracks. Huge ones, the biggest she'd ever seen. Tracks made within the past few minutes, judging by beads of water in the toes.

The mountain lion had just slaked its thirst.

Uncoiling, Winona spun. The pines that bordered the lake were quiet. Much *too* quiet. If she had not been so preoccupied, she would have noticed sooner. Automatically, her hand strayed to the knife on her hip. She wished she had brought a pistol or a rifle, but she hadn't anticipated trouble. That's what happened when someone grew complacent. When someone assumed they were safe when they were not.

Winona scanned the shore to the north and south. No small animals were to be found. No deer, either, and usually a few does boldly ventured from the brush at that time of day to drink.

It could only mean one thing. She had been inexcusably careless, inexcusably stupid.

Winona started toward the trail that linked the lake to the cabin. Hardly had she taken four steps when high grass off to the right parted and a great tawny head appeared. Winona froze again, her breath catching in her throat.

Feral eyes studied her with hungry intent. Slinking low to the ground, the panther commenced the telltale stalk of a cat that had selected its next meal. A black-tipped tail flicked above its hindquarters.

Winona slowly drew her knife. It was no match for the feline's razor-edged claws. But if she could wound it, if she could hold it at bay and yell her head off for help while retreating into the lake, she stood a chance. *If, if, if.*

Soundlessly, the cougar slunk forward another few feet. Its white muzzle framed by jutting whiskers, its devilish green eyes burning with hunger, the cat parted its mouth enough to expose fangs as wicked as any man-made weapon.

Winona backed up a step. Slowly, ever so slowly. To make

a sudden move invited a fierce onslaught. She opened her mouth to yell for those at the cabin when suddenly a gleeful girlish voice called out from a short distance up the trail.

"Ma! Ma! Are you down here?"

Pure fear clutched at Winona's heart. "Evelyn!" she cried. "Go back! Go back! Whatever you do, don't come any closer!"

The warning was too late. Out of the woods bounded a lithe antelope in mortal guise, a girl of nine, the spitting image of her mother attired in a similar buckskin dress. Her innocent face was creased in a warm smile. "What was that, Ma?"

"Please, no!" Winona breathed.

The cat had swiveled toward her child.

Evelyn King saw the stark horror on her mother's face, and turned. She didn't scream. Her mother had told her that to do so was a sign of cowardice, and a Shoshone must never be guilty of that. She didn't bolt, either, because her father had cautioned her against fleeing from a predator. In addition, they were Kings, and as her pest of a brother was so fond of saying, the King family never ran from anything.

Even so, Evelyn felt fright rip into her insides, and she wanted to run headlong back up the path. Clamping her teeth, she glanced at her feet for something she could use to protect herself. A fist-size rock lay to her left. Inching downward, she slowly reached for it.

The panther growled, low and ominous.

"Do not move!" Winona declared. All fear for her own safety was gone. She cared only about her daughter, only about the child she loved more than life itself. Blade leveled, she sidestepped, moving at a snail's pace, pausing between each step to gauge the mountain lion's reaction.

"Shouldn't we holler for help?" Evelyn asked.

"No." Winona had changed her mind. She was too afraid it might provoke the cougar into charging.

Evelyn didn't agree, but she trusted her mother's judgment.

Her mother always knew what was best. Well, almost always. And on those rare occasions when her mother didn't, her father did. Once, she had thought her parents knew everything. Both had since assured her there was much neither had ever learned.

That had been hard to grasp. If her folks, who were as near to perfect as it was humanly possible to be, did not know all there was worth knowing, then no one did, had, or ever would.

Winona watched the panther's tail. Should it stop twitching, should it suddenly go straight and stiff, it would signal an attack. The creature was glancing from her to Evelyn and back again as if it could not quite make up its mind which of them it wanted to eat. "Attack me," she said, gesturing.

Spitting, the mountain lion retreated a pace, then crouched lower.

It would not be long. And Winona had six feet to cover. Remembering the bucket, she swung it gently, the handle squeaking as would a mouse. It attracted the cat's attention. Continuing to swing, she warily sidestepped.

Evelyn heard a commotion up near the cabin. One loud outcry was all it would take to bring her uncle and the others rushing to the rescue. But her mother had said no, so that was that. She saw the big cat stare at her and shivered despite herself. Its eyes were cold, inhumanly cold. Yet at the same time they blazed with an inner fire. How that could be, she didn't know. They filled her with fear, fear that nearly made her head spin when the panther fixed its glare on her mother and took a half-step. "Ma?" she squeaked.

"Hush." Winona did not want to do anything that would invite a rush. But she was only fooling herself. When the cougar was ready, it would attack, and nothing she could do would forestall it.

The cat didn't like the squeaking. It slunk another few inches, then stopped and watched the bucket swing back and forth, growling ominously.

Winona swung faster, wider. If she could hold it at bay long enough to gain the footpath, Evelyn could race for the cabin. Extending her other arm, she looped it around her daughter's shoulders, careful not to poke Evelyn with the knife. "When I say so," she instructed, "run as you have never run before."

"You can count on me, Ma." Evelyn had smothered her fear by reminding herself that her mother would do whatever it took to spare her from harm. Then she had another thought, and the fear returned stronger than ever: Yes, her mother would protect her, but who would protect her mother?

The mountain lion didn't like being thwarted. Suddenly surging forward, it lashed out, a forepaw connecting with the bucket.

Winona nearly lost her hold. Had a claw snagged in the wood, she would have. As it was, her shoulder was horribly wrenched. She went on swinging, though, while steering her daughter closer to the trail.

As if it divined her intent, the painter bounded high into the air and alighted between the vegetation and them. Its tail swishing angrily, the cat vented a feral screech.

So much for that, Winona thought. "Into the lake!" she bawled, and gave her precious pride and joy a shove.

Caught flat-footed, Evelyn stumbled. She had to fling both arms out to keep from landing on her stomach. Her knees stung something awful. She raised her head—and there was the cougar, five feet away, steely legs coiling to spring.

Winona saw, too. "Nooooo!" she cried, aiming a swipe at the cat's face. Lightning reflexes saved it, and in retaliation the painter lashed out. This time those wicked curved claws bit deep into the bucket. Winona tugged—in vain. "Into the water! Hurry!"

The shout galvanized Evelyn into scrambling upright. The mountain lion released the bucket to dash at her. For an instant she figured she was dead. She imagined being torn open and feeling long fangs sink into her neck. But another swing of the bucket clipped the painter on the brow as it was rearing to pounce, and the predator recoiled

Too close, Winona's mind screamed. *Much too close!* She put herself in front of her offspring so the cat would have to get through her first. Not once did she stop swinging, for if she did so it would be on them in a heartbeat.

Evelyn barreled into the lake. A chill, damp sensation spread rapidly up her legs as she churned and flailed. All the splashing seemed to incite the mountain lion even more. It made a beeline for her, water or no.

Winona had both hands on the handle. She slammed the bucket against the cat's side, sparking another screech. Retreating to the water's edge, Winona aimed a terrific blow at the top of the cougar's skull, but it was too smart for her. It leaped to the left, well out of reach, and crouched in baffled frustration.

Water lapped at Winona's legs. She took another step and it rose above her ankles. Any farther in and she risked slipping. Planting both feet, she braced for the savage rush sure to come. She was not disappointed.

The panther had had enough. Snarling horribly, it came in fast and low. Water splashed up around its face and shoulders just as it cocked a forepaw. Spitting, it unexpectedly danced back onto shore.

A flicker of hope animated Winona. The cat didn't like to get wet! Grinning, she kicked out, sending a thick spray at the mountain lion's head. It hissed and backpedaled. Encouraged, she kicked again and again, harder and harder, driving it farther and farther back.

Evelyn laughed for joy. Just when she believed they did not stand a prayer, the cougar turned out to be scared of something as silly as water! Clapping, she hollered, "Go away! You mean coward!"

The cat growled menacingly. Beads of moisture dotted its whiskers, its jaw. In a molten streak it darted to the right as if to flee along the shoreline. Instead, in a twinkling, it turned and came at them, hips churning, tail straight.

Winona had barely set herself before the thing was on them. She did not waste more energy kicking water. The painter would not let anything short of death deter it again. She swung the bucket again. But in her haste she swung too soon. She missed, and before she could adjust, the cat was right there in front of her, a paw slashing at her midriff.

Winona threw herself backward. Her left foot slipped and down she went, onto her left knee. She wound up at eye level with the cougar, the bucket half in the lake, half out. The creature knew she was helpless. She could have sworn it smiled. Then it surged toward her.

"Ma!" Evelyn screamed. The cougar's tapered teeth were about to shear into her mother's neck, and in desperation Evelyn tried to get around past her mother to help.

Gleaming fangs filled Winona's line of vision. They seemed to fill the whole world, the whole firmament. Frantically, she shoved the bucket at its face—and connected. The bottom smashed into the cat's nose. In mindless fury it bit the bucket, its teeth lancing into the wood like spikes into tallow. The bucket was torn from her grasp.

Winona raised the knife, then paused. The cougar was backing away once more, tossing its head, and the bucket, from side to side. It took a moment for the reason to become apparent. The bucket was stuck! Somehow it had bitten so deep it couldn't get the bucket off! Under any other circumstances the comical outcome would have tickled her. But now she pivoted, grabbed her daughter's wrist, and made for solid ground.

Evelyn giggled hysterically. Never in all her life had she seen such a stupid cat. She couldn't believe she had been afraid of any animal so dumb! Struggling to keep up with her mother, she sprinted from the lake.

Winona angled toward the trail. Off through the pines lay

the cabin and salvation. Her rifles and her pistols were there. Nate had insisted she learn how to shoot years before. Subsequent events had proven the wisdom of his persistence, for she had lost track of the number of times it had saved her life.

The cat was in a berserk frenzy, leaping and snarling and tearing at the bucket. Landing on its back, it rolled against a boulder, the bucket smacking with a resounding *crack*. To Winona's consternation, the bucket tumbled loose. Immediately, the panther was erect and spinning.

They were so close! The trail mouth was a dozen steps away. Yet it might as well have been on the moon, since in two incredible bounds the cougar cut them off. Body crouched, tail whipping nonstop, it growled long and loud.

From the vicinity of the cabin yells arose in the Shoshone tongue. Someone had heard the commotion. Soon warriors would arrive. But would it be soon enough? Winona wondered as she speared the butcher knife at the beast's neck.

The mountain lion ducked, then sprang. Iron sinews that could propel it twenty feet in one jump now carried it up and over her arm, up and over the knife. Winona attempted to counter by twisting and impaling it in the stomach, but it was too swift.

Over two hundred and fifty pounds of tawny terror rammed into her. Raking forepaws caught her on the shoulders. She heard Evelyn screech as she was knocked flat on her back. Pain seared her arms, her chest. As well it should. For astride her was the cougar. It had her pinned.

Winona stared up into a contorted mask of icy-hearted blood lust. The cat had her at its mercy. Teeth glistened white. Saliva rimmed its lips. Its eyes swiveled to her exposed throat, to her jugular, and its mouth parted wider.

"Leave her be!"

Evelyn could never say why she did what she did. Most any other girl her age would have been too paralyzed. Small fists bunched, she went at the cat like a tiny bird protecting another. She punched its back, its side, and although she was much too young to inflict serious harm, she did cause it to turn and fix her with those baleful orbs.

"Leave my ma be!"

The cat was going to attack Evelyn! Winona pushed upward, the butcher knife cleaving in an overhand arc. Steel bit into flesh, rent sinew. In a flash, teeth sank into her right shoulder. Agony racked her from head to toe. She felt moisture on her skin and knew it was her own blood, oozing from the wound. The cougar had bit hard and was gnawing at her as it might on a large bone.

"Maaaaaa!" Evelyn pushed the cat, but it would not let go. Mind awhirl, she did the only thing she could think of. She dashed behind it and seized hold of its tail.

Winona felt strangely numb. She should be resisting tooth and nail, but a most peculiar lassitude afflicted her. When she felt the mountain lion's mouth release her shoulder, she attempted to rise, but her limbs refused to obey her will. As if in a haze, she saw the cat rise up and bend.

Resisting the numbness, Winona lifted her head a few inches. Dread without limit welled up within her. "Evelyn!" she breathed. "Run!"

Evelyn was not disposed to do any such thing. She yanked and yanked to force the cougar to get off, but the stubborn cat stood there regarding her more as a petty nuisance than anything else. "I won't let you hurt my ma again!"

The mountain lion uttered a high-pitched shriek, then reared with its front legs wide. Claws that could shred the thick hide of a shaggy buffalo were poised to do the same to the defenseless child.

Despite herself, Evelyn screamed and let go.

Winona screamed also. From the depths of her soul was wrung the anguished cry of a mother about to lose a child. No more heartrending sound is known, unless it's the wail of someone who has lost a sibling. She wailed and fought to scrabble upright. Traitor limbs hampered her, crumbling when she was only inches off the ground. "No! Please, no!" she railed.

For unendurable seconds the tableau was frozen. The mountain lion seemed suspended in midair. Evelyn was rigid, tiny fingers splayed to ward off the inevitable. Winona valiantly battled her lethargy, but her blood had the consistency of mud. Dully glittering claws began their descent.

A distinct thud brought the moment to an end. The cat's head jerked and its body was swatted as if by an invisible hand. It did an ungainly partial somersault, upending as it toppled so that it crashed to the earth facing her, mouth agape, tongue protruding. Confounded, Winona saw blood gush out over its tongue. She noted a hole on the side of its head, a neat hole rimmed by crimson.

Voices clamored. Forms materialized.

An elderly warrior whose hair and clothing marked him as a Shoshone had swept Evelyn into his arms and was examining her. Another warrior, younger and leaner, was sighting down an arrow at the prone painter. Yet a third Shoshone, a veritable giant seven feet tall, bent to help Winona stand. In his enormous grasp she was like an infant.

"Touch the Clouds! Thank you for saving us."

The renowned warrior grunted. "It was not I who shot."

She realized the giant didn't have a gun. Nor did either of the others. Yet she was positive a lead ball had brought the mountain lion down. "Then who—?"

Hammering hooves announced the arrival of someone else. A big black stallion was brought to a sliding halt and from the saddle flew a handsome, bearded white man whose skin had been so bronzed by the sun he could pass for an Indian himself. A smoking Hawken was in his right hand. Features aglow with love, he took her into his comforting arms.

"Husband!" Winona exclaimed.

Nate King had seldom been so petrified as when he emerged

from the forest across the lake and spotted his wife and daughter in fierce combat with the painter. He had bellowed for Zach and Shakespeare, who were bringing up the rear behind the greenhorns, then brought the stallion to a gallop and sped on around the lake as if outracing a prairie fire.

Nate had yelled himself hoarse trying to entice the cat to pay attention to him and not those who meant more to him than all the wealth the world had to offer, but neither the painter nor his wife or daughter heard.

He had taken a bead. But he was still out of range when the mountain lion bowled Winona over and bit her. Fuming in helpless rage, he had goaded the stallion to go faster when it was already going as fast as it could.

The Hawken swayed and bounced no matter how tightly he tucked it to his shoulder. Allowing the reins to fall, he guided the stallion by leg pressure alone. Simultaneously, he rose as high as he could for a clearer shot. His heart swelled with pride when he saw his daughter grip the panther's tail. And it just as instantaneously quaked with apprehension when the painter turned on her.

He had been too far away, even then. Too far, and unable to hold a steady bead, thanks to the stallion's rolling gait. Yet if he didn't shoot, if he didn't at least *try,* his daughter's life was forfeit.

So Nate had jammed the rifle hard against his arm, held his breath, lightly applied his finger to the trigger, then stroked it when the mountain lion reared. For unending moments he had watched in tense anticipation. Had he missed? Had he misjudged the angle and distance? Had he struck his wife or little girl by mistake? Would he spend the rest of his days in torment, racked by guilt?

The shot, though, had scored! Now Nate embraced his wife, holding her close. The scent of her hair was in his nostrils, the feel of her warm body the next best thing to heaven on earth. Thin arms wrapped around his leg and he looked down into the upturned face of a perfect cherub.

"Pa! You're back! Was that you who saved us?"

Nate could only smile and swallow the lump in his throat. Raising Evelyn to his shoulder, he gave her the same treatment while thanking his Maker for their deliverance.

"Can't you speak?" Evelyn asked, and giggled. "Cat got your tongue?"

Winona gave voice to a partial laugh, partial soul-tearing sob. Of all the many perils they had faced, this one had come closest to doing her in. Which reminded her. She drew back to inspect her wound, but Nate misconstrued and planted his hungry lips on her mouth.

Evelyn looked at Spotted Bull, who winked playfully. One of the oldest living Shoshones, he was a special favorite of hers. He liked to tell stories and spoil her with gifts. A doll she adored more than any other had been a present from him and his wife, Morning Dove, the sister of her mother's mother.

At that juncture another of Evelyn's favorites galloped up. "Uncle Shakespeare!" she squealed.

The mountain man radiated relief. "Thank God!" Dismounting, he took her from her father. "Bring me the fairest creature northward born that I might shower her with affection!"

Nate straightened and saw a dark stain on his wife's dress. "Damn," he said, seeing the bite and claw marks clearly. Some were deep. He bent to examine them, but her stern expression and a restraining hand on his wrist stopped him. She was scrutinizing the New Yorkers.

"What have we here, husband?" Winona asked, reproach in her tone. Almost to herself, she repeated, "What have we here?"

Chapter Eight

"They're Indians."

"Shoshones, to be exact."

Isaiah Tompkins blinked at the veritable giant who regarded him inscrutably. Touch the Clouds, his host had called him. "They're *savages*."

Nate King controlled his temper with an effort. "They are my family and friends. And I won't abide having them insulted. Remember that."

Verbal flint grated on cold steel. Isaiah saw fingers of fire blaze in the mountain man's simmering eyes and recalled Shakespeare McNair's warning. "I didn't mean to offend you. It's just that, well, they *are* Indians. So I can't help but feel a little nervous."

Nate sighed. Relatively few whites had ever actually met an Indian, yet most were scared to death of them. Lurid horror tales of gruesome atrocities supposedly perpetrated by the red race were to blame. That, and the U.S. government's own unofficial but widely publicized policy to the effect that the only really good Indians were those who had been forcibly removed from white lands. Or were dead.

Rufus Stern had an urge to slap his partner silly. What was Isaiah thinking? They desperately needed the trapper's aid if they were to ever see wonderful civilization again. The last thing they should do was antagonize him. "Yes. Please forgive Isaiah," he interjected. "I'm sure we'll get along just fine with your—er—acquaintances."

Shakespeare McNair could not help but overhear, and sighed. "Young gentlemen," he commented, "your spirits are too bold for your years. You have seen cruel proof of this man's strength. If you saw yourself with your eyes, or knew yourself with your judgment, the fear of your adventure would counsel you to a more equal enterprise."

Rufus deemed it sage advice. "Please. Honest. We'll be on our best behavior the whole time we're here. You can trust us."

Nate wanted to, he truly did, but he had his family to think of. Mixing the greenhorns and the Shoshones was like mixing axle grease and water. The two would never blend perfectly. He looked at his wife, who had not uttered a word the whole trek up the trail to their cabin, and who now stood regarding the newcomers much as she might a roving silvertip griz. "They were stranded," he explained. "Either I helped them or they died."

"No need to explain, husband," Winona responded. There was no denying her man had a kind heart. It was one of the traits that first attracted her to him. But kindness extended blindly sometimes reaped more heartbreak than happiness. A few years ago Nate had brought home another lost pair, a treacherous couple who had tried to slay their whole family.

Isaiah sensed the outcome hinged on the woman's decision. Her beauty shocked him. She was the most exquisite female he had ever set eyes on. And as a rake and a rogue, he should know, having wooed more than his fair share. So lovely was she, he had to be careful not to ogle her in front of her husband. Adopting a suave smile, he said earnestly, "We beseech you, madam. Take pity on us. All of this is so new, so exceptional, we're having a hard time adjusting. But I give you my solemn word that Rufus and I will never deliberately do anything to hurt you or yours."

Winona hesitated. Her natural impulse to protect her loved ones warred with her compassion for those in need. "Very well," she said reluctantly. "You may stay. But only until you are ready to travel again."

Isaiah was so elated, he almost hugged her. "You won't regret your decision, I assure you," he pledged while admiring the silken sheen to Winona's luxurious raven tresses.

Rufus was equally delighted. The sturdy cabin in which the Kings lived reminded him of an uncle's in upstate New York. He couldn't wait to sleep indoors again! To have a roof over his head to ward off the elements and four stout walls to keep out predators and whatnot. He took a step toward the doorway.

"You can set up a lean-to yonder," Nate King said, pointing to the north. The lodges of his Shoshone visitors were to the south. He felt it best to keep them separated.

"Lean-to?" Rufus said, crestfallen.

Shakespeare chuckled. "I'll show you how to make one. It'll keep you as dry and snug as two peas in a pod. Used one myself many a time." Clapping Stern on the shoulders, he said, "Come hither, man. I see that thou art poor."

Rufus did not see what his lack of funds had to do with anything. Yes, he was poor, or he wouldn't have agreed to Isaiah's silly quest to reap a fortune in beaver hides. He allowed the grizzled mountain man to steer him toward a stand of pines.

Isaiah tore his gaze from Winona King and followed. Finding her so attractive bothered him. She was an Indian, and everyone knew Indians were little better than animals. The clergy called them heathens. The government branded them as vermin worthy of extermination. Why, even his own father liked to refer to them as "red scum." So how in the name of all that was holy could he find himself attracted to one?

Nate King turned to his other visitors. Spotted Bull was his wife's uncle. Touch the Clouds and Drags the Rope were two of his best friends. Beyond reared their three lodges. Their wives were off gathering roots, he had been told. "I thank you for coming to Winona's assistance," he said soberly in the Shoshone tongue.

Spotted Bull's wrinkled visage acquired more creases. "What else would we do? Let the cat kill her? I do not want to lose my favorite niece any more than you want to lose the heart you treasure more than your own."

Nate smiled. The ancient one had a flair for colorful speech rivaling Shakespeare's.

Drags the Rope nodded at the horses. "Your hunt was unsuccessful?"

"Not through any fault of ours," Nate responded, then proceeded to relate details. Everyone had been counting on some fresh buffalo meat after weeks of venison. The panther would be a nice change of pace, but there wasn't enough to last very long. "Looks as if I'll have to head out in the morning after elk or bear."

"We will do the hunting," Touch the Clouds said. "You must stay to keep watch over the whites."

Ever since the Shoshones had adopted Nate into his tribe, they always referred to him as one of their own. He was no longer a white man in their eyes. And, truth to tell, at times he *felt* more Indian than white. "I would be grateful."

Unnoticed at the corner of the cabin, Zachary King stared after the would-be trappers and scowled in disapproval. His parents were much more considerate than he would be. Were it up to him, he'd have left the pair on the prairie to perish or survive on their own. He owed them nothing. They were strangers. Worse, they were *white*, and hard experience had taught him the majority of his father's people weren't to be trusted. Most looked down their noses at him. He was a *'breed,* the offshoot of a white father and a red mother. Somehow, that made him inferior, made him the butt of contempt and scorn. When he was younger he had tolerated the hatred, but no more. He was on the threshold of manhood. And as a man, he would suffer no abuse.

Zach was about to turn and take his horse to the corral when he saw Isaiah Tompkins glance over a shoulder. At his mother. For a fleeting instant Zach registered something peculiar in the New Yorker's eyes. Something he could not quite identify. Then Thomas spied him and quickly faced front.

What was that all about? Zach asked himself as he grasped the roan's reins and walked off. He could not say exactly why, but it troubled him. He made a mental note to keep a close eye on the pair. Let his father treat them as brothers. They weren't *his.*

Nate held the cabin door open for his wife and daughter. "Let's tend those wounds," he suggested.

Winona let him have his way. She made no comment as he tenderly cleaned the claw marks and the deeper punctures made by the cougar's sharp teeth. Not once did she flinch or so much as bat an eyelid.

His wife's silence troubled Nate. She was upset but trying not to show it. So was he, at how closely she had come to being slain. The bite on her shoulder had seared into the flesh as if it were so much soft wax. Any deeper and she would have been crippled for life. Using a soft cloth soaked in tincture, he carefully applied a wide bandage. "I'll change this every eight hours or so until the danger is passed."

Winona nodded. Festering infection must be scrupulously avoided. Once it set in, it was next to impossible to curb. Many a Shoshone had lived through a fierce battle or brutal animal attack only to fall prey to putrid poison in the blood.

Finishing, Nate bent lower and kissed her on the forehead.

"I'm sorry. Honest to goodness. I didn't know what else to do with them."

"I forgive you." Winona observed her daughter playing with a doll over by the stone fireplace. "I just wish it had not happened now, of all times."

"Shakespeare and I won't let them out of our sight. There won't be any trouble. I give you my word."

Evelyn approached bearing her doll. A gift from a missionary's wife, it was a fine miniature of a white woman in a long dress and bonnet. Her favorite. She liked it even more than the one Spotted Bull's wife had given her, a perfect likeness of a Shoshone woman complete with a cradleboard and tiny infant on its back. "Can we invite Mr. Tompkins and Mr. Stern for supper, Ma?"

"If you want," Winona answered.

"I do," Evelyn said, grinning. "They can tell us all about life in the place they come from. In a big city."

Winona's lips pinched together. Her daughter's growing fondness for the white way of life was mildly unsettling. She had always taken it for granted Evelyn would one day wed a prominent Shoshone warrior, not a white man. It shouldn't make a difference, though, since *she* had taken a white man as a mate. But deep down, it did. "We will invite them, then."

"Good!" Evelyn clapped her slender hands. "I can ask what all the ladies do." She never tired of hearing the latest about white women. At the last rendezvous she had talked her mother into visiting a party of what her uncle Shakespeare called "Bible-thumpers" to badger the minister's wife with questions.

"Just so you do not make a pest of yourself."

"Never, Ma. I'll be real polite."

Nate was at a counter, washing his hands in a basin. He reckoned it was all right for the New Yorkers to come. The sooner they made plans to send the pair on their way, the better off for everyone.

Isaiah Tompkins dreamed. He was alone in a pristine field of golden flowers. Out of a shimmering rosy haze appeared a silhouette, a figure that ran toward him with outstretched arms. A figure that resolved itself into the spitting image of Winona King. Her long hair flew in the wind and she had a warm smile of greeting on her red lips. Isaiah flung his arms wide to receive her. But she ran right on past him, past him and into the arms of her husband, Nate.

Isaiah swore under his breath as they passionately kissed. He yearned to be sharing her embrace and imagined sweet sensations rippling through him. A rocking motion broke the spell, a motion he couldn't account for until he suddenly opened his eyes and found Rufus's hand on his shoulder.

"Nap time is over, partner. We're due at the Kings' shortly."

Yawning, Isaiah sat up. His head nearly brushed the top of the lean-to they had erected under Shakespeare McNair's guidance.

"What were you dreaming about?" Rufus asked.

"I can't recall," Isaiah lied. "Why?"

"You were groaning and moaning as if you were in seventh heaven." Rufus laughed. "Remembering one of your many lusty wenches, were you? Maybe that one who was partial to dressing all in red?" His friend's fondness for women—*all* women—had always amused him. "Or was it that one who liked to suck on your tongue?"

Isaiah vented brittle mirth. Inexplicably, the jest angered him. Even more so since he immediately thought of Winona King. "Must have been one I'm quite fond of, but I can't remember which."

"You? Fond of any one woman?" Rufus laughed louder. "No female in her right mind would tie her apron strings to you unless she was a glutton for punishment."

"What the hell does that mean?" Isaiah snapped before he

could stop himself. "I'd make as fine a husband as you would,
I'll have you know. Better, since I'm not half as naive or a
third as gullible."

The venom his friend oozed startled Rufus. Isaiah's lack of
interest in marriage had long been a private joke between
them. "Don't work yourself into a dither. One day some poor
gal will come along and let you sweep her off her feet. More's
the pity." Rufus playfully nudged Isaiah to show he was poking fun.

"Let's get ready."

Isaiah dismissed the incident from his mind. He also tried
to forget about his dream. But the sight of Winona King, ra-
diant in a resplendent buckskin dress adorned with bright blue
beads, literally took his breath away. Entranced, he barely
heard her greeting, or the remarks Nate made as they were
invited to sit at a table fitted with a genuine tablecloth.

It got worse. Isaiah could tear his eyes from her only with
a struggle. Her every movement was grace personified. Her
laughter was exquisite music. He feasted on her beauty rather
than the food, casting secret glances when no one was apt to
catch on—which was not nearly often enough to suit him. He
had to exercise supreme caution, with Zach King and Shakespeare also present.

McNair was in a spirited frame of mind. He entertained
them by quoting from *As You Like It*. Isaiah, enrapt, barely
heard four words until a quote perked his interest.

". . . when Nature hath made a fair creature, may she not
by Fortune fall into the fire? Though nature hath given us wit
to flout at Fortune, hath not Fortune sent in this fool to cut
off the argument?" Changing his voice to mimic a woman's,
Shakespeare assumed the part of Rosalind. "Indeed, there is
Fortune too hard for Nature, when Fortune makes Nature's
natural the cutter-off of Nature's wit."

Rufus chortled, more at the mountain man's excellent mimicry than the quote, which he would be the first to admit he didn't fully comprehend.

"Peradventure this is not Fortune's work neither, but Nature's. Who perceiveth our natural wits too dull to reason of such goddesses, and hath sent this natural for our whetstone. For always the dullness of the fool is the whetstone of the wits. How now, wit! Whither wander you?"

Rufus reached for his tin cup, then froze. He had witnessed a stolen glance thrown by his friend at their host's wife. A glance that could not be mistaken for anything other than what it was. It could not be! It simply could not be!

Overlooked by the adults, Zachary King sat in the rocking chair by the fireplace, as outwardly impassive as the stones behind him. Inwardly he seethed, for he had not taken his eyes off of Isaiah Tompkins once all evening, although he had *appeared* to. Young he might be, but not so young that the significance of the white man's secretive antics were lost on him. If not for the conviction his ma and pa would deem it bad manners, he'd have pulled out his butcher knife and buried the blade in the white man's back with no qualms whatsoever.

"The more pity," Shakespeare was saying, "that fools may not speak wisely what wise men do foolishly."

A bell reverberated in Isaiah's skull. He was being a fool himself, to think romantically of a heathen. That she was another man's wife was of little consequence. Since she was a heathen, the legality of her marital status was questionable at best.

For the longest while Isaiah daydreamed about taking her with him back to New York. He flattered himself that with a change of clothes and some lessons in etiquette, he could make a new woman out of her. A white woman, as it were. Another quote brought his reverie to an end.

"Is it possible that on so little acquaintance you should like her? That but seeing you should love her? And loving, woo?

111

And, wooing, she should grant? And will you persevere to enjoy her?''

The seed of an idea sprouted in Isaiah's brain. An idea at once fantastical and ridiculous. An idea so riveting, his breath caught in his throat and his pulse quickened. He would have to be insane to carry it out. Yet when he stared anew at Winona's ravishing features, at her sensational bronzed complexion and the shapely fit of her dress, a stirring in his loins echoed a stirring in his core. Impossibly enough, he wanted this woman as he had never wanted any woman, ever. And—dared he even think it?—*he meant to have her.*

Nate King was listening to his mentor, enjoying the recital. Brawny arms folded, he resisted a temptation to doze now and then. A full belly, the presence of his loved ones, being safe at home, all these factors conspired to fill him with pleasant contentment.

Nate's chin was on his chest when a small hand slipped into his. Rousing, he hoisted his daughter onto his lap. She snuggled warmly against his chest and whispered, ''When will Uncle Shakespeare be done so I can ask about the ladies?''

McNair was about to launch into an appropriate part. Winking at Nate, he quoted, ''I will weary you then no longer with idle talking. Know of me then, for now I speak to some purpose, that I know you are a gentleman of good conceit.'' Leaning back, he clasped his hands. ''Ask away, sprite. Far be it from me to stand in the way of acquiring knowledge.''

''Are you talking to me, Uncle?'' Evelyn asked.

''If there be truth in sight, you are my daughter.''

''Huh?''

Evelyn adored her uncle dearly, but he had a knack for confusing her terribly. Rather than attempt to sort it out, she beamed at their guests and gushed, ''Please tell us about New York City. What are the ladies there wearing? What do they like to do?''

Isaiah waved a hand. ''Ask my friend, child. He would

know better than I, since he was engaged to be married.''

''Oh, you were?'' Evelyn addressed Rufus. ''What is she like? Tell us all about her.''

''I don't know . . .'' Rufus balked. Discussing his beloved in front of anyone was taxing enough; some matters were too personal. But he could and did describe the type of dresses worn by Agnes and her friends, and the entertainments they enjoyed.

Evelyn listened with vibrant interest. Based on the stories she had heard, she pictured white women as living lives of magnificent splendor. Instead of simple hide lodges, they lived in stately homes. Instead of dirt floors, they had polished wood or plush carpet underfoot. Instead of buckskins they wore fancy dresses made of fantastic materials. They rode around in fine carriages pulled by sleek horses. Days were spent in carefree chats, nights were devoted to the theater and social get-togethers.

To Evelyn's way of thinking, white women had a much better life than the women of her mother's tribe. She would rather spend her days sipping tea and her evenings out on the town than spend her days skinning buffalo hides and her evenings slaving over a steaming cook pot.

But Evelyn had never admitted how she felt to anyone. She sensed it would upset her mother greatly, and Evelyn loved her mother too dearly to ever want to hurt her.

Unknown to the girl, Winona already knew. The persistent questions, the obvious excitement when the subject was raised, persuaded Winona her pride and joy had more interest in the white world than the red. It saddened her, but she didn't make an issue of it. Shoshones raised children to think for themselves. So whatever course Evelyn's life took must be Evelyn's to decide.

The candle on the table suddenly flickered when a gusty breeze swept in through the opened door. Drags the Rope was framed in the doorway. "Touch the Clouds and I hunt elk at sunrise," he announced.

"Spotted Bull does not want to go along?" Nate quipped. For someone who had seen over seventy winters, the venerable warrior was as spry as a youth in the prime of life.

Drags the Rope smiled. "He does. But Touch the Clouds says he must stay and protect our families."

Protect them from whom? Nate was going to ask, and saw his friend's eyes dart to the greenhorns.

"Will you join us, Grizzly Killer? Or you, Carcajou?"

Shakespeare chortled. *Some choice.* He could spend long hours in the saddle tracking wary elk into dense thickets where sharp limbs poked and prodded without mercy. Or he could stay at the cabin and while away the day not doing much of anything except playing with Evelyn and treating himself to Winona's sweet cakes. "Reckon you can manage without me," he said with a straight face.

For Nate the decision was not so easy. As the one who had invited the Shoshones to his valley, he was obligated to ensure they were well fed during their stay. On the other hand, leaving his family while the New Yorkers were there did not appeal to him. Torn by indecision, he gnawed on his lower lip.

Shakespeare had not acquired so many white hairs by dipping his head in bleach. Winking at Nate, he commented, "Fret not, Horatio. I'll watch over things here while you're gone."

"I don't want to impose . . ." Nate began.

"Oh, please." Shakespeare gestured. "Why, right. You are in the right. And so, without more circumstance at all, I hold it fit that we shake hands and part. You, as your business and desire shall point you. For every man hath business and desire, such as it is. For my own, poor part, look you, I'll go pray." Rising, he exited the cabin, his merry mirth wafting on the wind.

"What an eccentric character," Rufus remarked.

"Eccentric? Or mad?" Isaiah said. "Seems to me there's a fine line between the two, and your friend, King, has crossed over it."

Nate would have risen in resentment had Evelyn not been perched on his knee. "That madman, as you call him, has been more like a father to me than my real father. You would be better off, friend, if some of his madness rubbed off on you."

Isaiah casually looked at Winona, then just as casually looked away. "I beg your pardon. I do believe you have a point."

Rufus stood and tugged on his companion's sleeve. "I believe we've imposed on these kind people enough. My thanks, Mrs. King, for the delicious meal. I haven't eaten so good since we left St. Louis."

Evelyn hopped off her father. "You're welcome to join us tomorrow, too," she cheerfully offered. "Aren't they, Ma?"

Winona had no desire to invite them again, but she couldn't deny her daughter. "Yes. By all means. Tomorrow night."

Rufus was about to decline. Once was enough of an imposition. But Isaiah surprised him by venturing, "We'll be delighted, Mrs. King. Wouldn't miss it for the world." Pushing his chair back, he smiled at each of the Kings as he rose. Only the girl returned it. Nate merely nodded. Winona showed no emotion. As for the boy—Zachary gave Isaiah such a spiteful look that it slapped Isaiah with the force of a physical blow.

The moment passed so quickly that Isaiah half doubted it had happened. Puzzled, he opened the door for his friend and strolled out into the brisk night air. The scent of burning wood tingled his nose. From the vent holes at the peaks of the three tepees rose spiraling smoke. In one of them a woman hummed loudly.

Rufus fell into step beside Isaiah. "What was that all about back there?"

"Can you elaborate?"

"Don't play me for a fool. I know you too well. And I saw

the look you gave Winona King. What are you up to?''

"Not a thing," Isaiah said innocently.

Much too innocently, Rufus reflected. "I hope for your sake that you're telling the truth. This isn't New York. Trifle with Winona and Nate will gut you like a fish."

Isaiah didn't respond, which only worried Rufus more.

Chapter Nine

Touch the Clouds and Drags the Rope were waiting when Nate King quietly slipped from the still cabin shortly before daybreak. Both Shoshones wore buckskins, and each had brought a bow and a quiver full of arrows.

It took only a few minutes for Nate to throw his saddle and bridle on the stallion and secure a parfleche filled with his possibles. After looping a lead rope around a trio of packhorses, he was ready to depart.

His friends let him lead the way. It was his valley, his domain. He knew it better than they, knew the haunts of the elk and deer and other creatures that shared his home. Nate rode to the northwest, toward emerald slopes thick with firs and aspens.

No one spoke. Such carelessness would be unforgivable. Nate had cleared the valley of predators, but others, like the mountain lion, often passed through, and always there was the danger of stumbling on a hostile war party.

Not that the woods were quiet. Quite the contrary. Birds

broke into a full-throated avian chorus to herald the rising of the sun. Squirrels awoke to chatter irritably at the intruders below, or to scamper playfully through the upper terrace. Chipmunks chittered and flitted among boulders. Occasional deer either bolted for cover or stood watching the riders in perfect natural innocence.

Nate King breathed deep of the pine-scented chill air and thanked his Maker for his own private slice of Eden. Nate *loved* the wilderness.

A grunt from Touch the Clouds drew Nate's attention. To the west a bobcat was bounding into cover. A rare treat, since by nature bobcats were extremely reclusive.

Drags the Rope pointed to the north where a lone bald eagle soared majestically on the currents high above pristine peaks. A good omen, he thought. Eagles were always good omens. It hinted their hunt would be successful. He took the liberty of mentioning as much.

"Hope you're right," Nate said.

Touch the Clouds had nothing to say. Everyone was aware of his outlook on omens. To believe in them was silly. That eagle, for instance, was simply hunting for food. There was no hidden meaning.

Touch the Clouds had always been unique among his people. Even as a child, when he had been twice as big and three times as strong as boys his age.

Inside, he had been different, too. Unlike his brothers and sisters, he had questioned everything. When an elder told him something, he always had to prove it was true before he would believe it himself.

His outlook on omens was typical. His people were always looking for sign and portents, always seeking guidance, always striving to unravel the secrets of the Great Mystery. To him it was a monumental waste.

Life happened. The majestic flight of an eagle was just that, nothing more. When a prairie wolf crossed your path, it was a coincidence. It did not mean someone you knew was going to fall ill.

Touch the Clouds often wondered why he was so unlike his brethren. He concluded his size was the main factor. Early on in life he had learned to rely on himself to the exclusion of all else, to depend on his rippling sinews to spare him from diverse dangers.

An eagle soaring on high would not save a man from a hungry grizzly. But that man's limbs could—with the help of a gun or a bow.

The howl of a wolf would not save someone from roving enemies. But strong arms and a brave heart could.

Omens were for those who had not learned to accept the world for the way it really was. For those who preferred to have their steps directed by unseen forces. For those who had never outgrown the need to constantly look up to a parent for guidance.

Touch the Clouds stared at the eagle, wishing it would venture lower. He needed a new supply of feathers for his arrows.

Presently the hunters reached the lower edge of the green slopes, slopes that would eventually bring them to a particular meadow. A meadow where elk congregated to graze. If they could reach it before the heat of the day drove the herd into shaded timber, they could bring one down, carve it up, and be back at the cabin only a few hours after nightfall.

Nate felt guilty about leaving his family alone with the New Yorkers. He would never have done so except for his unbounded confidence in his mentor. Shakespeare would look after them as competently as he would; better, even.

He had nothing to worry about.

Isaiah Tompkins had hardly slept a wink all night. Try as he might—and he didn't try very hard—he could not stop thinking about Winona King.

He told himself he was being silly. The only reason he gave

the squaw any notice at all were the long weeks spent on the prairie. The long, lonely weeks without female companionship.

Isaiah had always liked the fairer sex. Rufus teased him no end about the steady stream of beauties he dated, but Rufus was envious. Could Isaiah help it if he'd been blessed with good looks and an abundance of charm and wit?

It had not been hard for Isaiah to leave his family. It hadn't been difficult for him to bid adieu to his friends. But giving up the nightlife of New York City, and the dazzling women who made that nightlife so richly enjoyable, had been a true test of his mettle.

Isaiah had never gone so long without tasting feminine delights. He sorely missed their laughter, their wit, their buxom bodies pulsing for his hungry touch. They had been practically all he thought about while crossing the damnable plain. Until the horses were stolen.

So his infatuation with the Shoshone woman had to be the result of his yearning. That, and nothing more. Yet knowing the truth did not dispel his craving. If anything, he craved her *more*.

Talk about stupid. While Isaiah had trifled with married women on occasion, one look at Nate King was enough to give any rake second thoughts.

Some husbands meekly accepted being put upon. They might rant at their wives if their spouses were caught being unfaithful, but they were too cowardly to confront their rivals. Other husbands, the ones Isaiah avoided, were just as liable to wring a rogue's neck.

Nate King was in a class all by himself. Isaiah could easily picture the mountain man whipping out that long butcher knife and gutting anyone who dared look crosswise at Winona. Without batting an eye.

But Isaiah couldn't help himself. He couldn't stop dreaming about her, about her supple movements, her white even teeth, her red rosy lips. About the halo of vibrant beauty she radiated.

What was happening to him?

Childish mirth intruded on Isaiah's troubled musing. Over by the cabin Shakespeare McNair was swinging little Evelyn, and she was giddy with glee. Close by, Winona and an older Shoshone looked on, smiling. Isaiah was enticed by how amply Winona filled out the top of her buckskin dress, how the dress jiggled when she laughed. A lump formed in his throat. His skin prickled as if from a heat rash.

"Stop it, damn you."

Rufus had come from the bushes. Isaiah's expression was all too familiar, a look of raw lust Rufus had seen on innumerable occasions.

"I don't know what you're talking about," Isaiah said sullenly.

"Liar." Rufus took a seat under the lean-to, crossing his legs as he sank down. He had almost forgotten about the incident the night before. All morning he had been roving the area, enjoying the splendor, the invigorating crisp mountain air. "I won't warn you again. You're playing with fire. It's bad enough you carry on with married women the same as you do with single women. But *now? Here?* Do you have a death wish? If Nate King doesn't slit your throat, any one of those savages gladly would."

Isaiah resented being lectured. "There's no harm in a man admiring a fine figure of a woman."

"There is when the woman has given herself to someone else and your admiration is plain for anyone to see." Rufus thought of his sweet, loyal Agnes. She'd box his ears if he ever ogled another female.

"I can do what I want. Keep your nose out of it."

"Now you sound like a ten-year-old," Rufus said. "Sure, any of us can do what we please. But we had better be willing to pay the price. Are you?" When Isaiah didn't reply, Rufus continued. "Need I remind you that if not for Nate King, we wouldn't ever see New York again?'' Still his partner sat stubbornly silent. "Damn, Isaiah. King has been good enough to take us in, feed us, protect us. And this is how you repay him?''

"I haven't done anything.''

"Not yet. But I know you. I know how you think. You're trying to figure out how to have your way with Winona without losing your life.''

"I am not," Isaiah responded testily. Though, the truth be known, he had been contemplating that very thing.

"I'm telling you here and now, I want no part of it. Whatever you do, you're on your own. I won't back you up.''

"Did I ask you to?''

Rufus had more to say, but just then he thought that he heard something to his left, off in the pines. No animals were evident, not so much as a chirping bird. Yet he was positive he had heard the faintest of noises. He started to swivel his head when a shadowy shape flitted across a shaded patch, a brief flicker of movement that brought Rufus to his feet, his nerves on edge.

Isaiah stirred. "What is it?''

"I don't know. An animal, I guess. A big one.''

Standing, Isaiah retrieved his rifle. Their host claimed the valley was the safest spot in the Rockies. But King's own wife had nearly been ripped to shreds by that cougar. "I don't see anything.''

For tense moments the two of them waited for a creature to appear.

"Rosencrantz! Gildenstern! What bodes you ill? You have the aspect of men about to be consumed by their own fears.'' Shakespeare McNair sauntered to the lean-to. "Angels and ministers of grace defend us! Be thou a spirit of health or goblin damned, bring with thee airs from heaven or blasts from hell, be thy intents wicked or charitable, thou comest in such a questionable shape that I will speak to thee.''

Isaiah had had just about enough of the old man's relentless raving. "You fool. There's something in the trees."

"You don't say?" Shakespeare rested a hand on one of his pistols and moved to the tree line. A fly buzzed by him. A bee droned among flowers.

Rufus moved forward. "Honestly. I saw it myself."

"To be honest, as this world goes, is to be one man picked out of ten thousand." Shakespeare quoted again one of his favorite lines.

"Huh?" Rufus did not see what that had to do with the situation. "I wouldn't go in there, were I you. Not until we know what it is."

"My fate cries out, and makes each petty artery in this body as hardy as the Nemean lion's nerve." So declaring, Shakespeare jerked his pistol and marched into the cool murk of the heavy growth. Here the trees grew so close together and were so tall, they blocked out most of the sunlight.

Rufus was loath to follow, but his conscience would not let him let the oldster face the creature alone. "Contrary joker," he muttered, sidling into the growth as if into a wall of crackling flames.

"A fellow of infinite jest, of most excellent fancy," Shakespeare quipped. His razor-honed instincts gave assurance all was tranquil. As he'd suspected. Greenhorns had a tendency to imagine monsters where none existed. "So where, exactly, did you see whatever it was?"

Pointing, Rufus said, "Right about there. I didn't get much of a look. Sorry."

"We should never apologize for our shortcomings," Shakespeare said. "We should correct them." Stepping to the side of a regal tree, he gazed upward the length of the towering trunk, then down at the ground.

"What is it?" Rufus asked. The mountain man's brow had knit.

"Just some rabbit tracks," Shakespeare fibbed. For there

was only one print, the partial scuff mark of a moccasin, so indistinct that Stern would be blind to its presence. Its size gave Shakespeare a clue to the maker's identity. Puzzlement grew.

"That's all? What I saw was no rabbit. It was big, I tell you."

"Could have been anything," Shakespeare said, turning. "A deer. A trick of the wind and sunlight." Shoving the pistol under his belt, he chuckled. "Many a time I've been scared half out of my paltry wits by a wayward shadow."

"You? I didn't think you knew the meaning of fear."

"Ah. Fright and I are old acquaintances. But I've learned to slam the door in his face when he shows up. Denial is the best antidote for a yellow backbone."

Rufus was glad they were safe. He pivoted to rejoin Isaiah—but Isaiah was gone. Rufus surveyed the clearing and the woodland. "Now, where the devil did that fool get to?" he commented.

Shakespeare was on his way to the cabin. He detoured when Zachary King emerged from the forest a stone's throw away. "Young Troilus, a word with you, if you please." Zach slowed and Shakespeare paced him, clasping his hands behind his back. "I realize it's none of my business, Stalking Coyote. But I'm curious as to why you've been spying on our guests."

Zach feigned interest at Long's Peak. "Why would I bother? I have better things to do with my time."

Shakespeare was sincerely shocked. They had always been the best of friends. Many an evening he had read from the bard for the boy's enjoyment, or recounted tales of his own exploits. To his knowledge, Zach had never lied to him—or been so blatantly evasive as the boy was being now.

"If I knew why, I wouldn't need to ask."

"Do you like them, Uncle?"

The blunt question was typical of youth. Direct and to the point. Shakespeare picked his words with as much care as he would pick berries from a thorny stem. "I don't *dislike* them, son, if that's what you're getting at. They're green as grass and have mud for brains, but they haven't done anything to earn my hatred. I'll be glad when we're shed of them, though."

Zachary studied the man who was more like a grandfather to him than a family friend. "You taught me never to judge a man by the color of his skin or the clothes he wears. Remember?"

Shakespeare smirked. "I seem to recollect spouting off about a great many things. Yes."

"So I was willing to give them the benefit of the doubt. Even after the dark one tried to shoot me just because he thought I was an Indian."

"Stupidity is a common affliction," Shakespeare joked.

"Now I *hate* him."

The intensity of the statement disturbed McNair. "Lord, son. If being stupid was cause for hating, the human race would have wiped itself out ages ago."

"I hate him," Zach repeated.

"Mind telling me why?"

Zach wanted to. But no one else had seen the glance Thomas gave his mother. They would say he was making a mountain out of a molehill, as the saying went. But he knew what he had seen, he knew what it meant.

"I'll keep it a secret just between the two of us," Shakespeare coaxed. He figured it had something to do with the boy's resentment toward all whites for how they generally treated half-breeds. 'Breeds were widely despised, their only "crime" being their mixed ancestry. Highly unfair, but then, life was often unfair. Even cruel.

Zach was inclined to open up. He halted and turned. Then he saw Isaiah Tompkins in the brush, staring toward the cabin. In front of it his mother chatted with Morning Dove. A cold chill blew through him and his stomach balled into a knot.

"Yes?"

"You're imagining things, Uncle. I wasn't spying on them."

"Tell that to your tracks. I saw where you eavesdropped from behind that big fir. But you were sloppy. Stern spotted you."

Anger was to blame. Zach had been so mad on hearing Tompkins accused of "wanting to have his way" with his mother that he had spun and left before he did a rash and violent act. Numbed by rage, he had almost given himself away.

"What's it all about, son?" Shakespeare rested a hand on the youth's bony shoulder. "You can confide in me. Haven't we always been the best of friends? Who kept it a secret when you lost your pa's folding knife? And who kept his mouth shut about that duck you bashed by mistake when you were chucking rocks?"

"I—" Zach began, still observing Isaiah Tompkins. The man licked his lips as might someone about to partake of a delicious feast. Fire burned through Zach's veins, and for a few seconds the world spun.

"What?"

"Never mind. It's nothing."

Abruptly, Zach wheeled and stalked westward, past the cabin, well beyond it and into another belt of pines. He had to put some distance between him and the greenhorns. He had get away or one of them would not live out the day.

"Zach?" Shakespeare called, to no avail.

Winona heard the shout and pivoted.

"You should see what that is about," Morning Dove advised. Having raised five children of her own, she was experienced at recognizing trouble.

The forest swallowed Zach. Shakespeare hurried to overtake him, but the hot-tempered youth was nowhere to be found when Shakespeare reached the vegetation. "Damn," he said under his breath.

"What is wrong with Stalking Coyote?"

Shakespeare averted Winona's probing gaze as he raked the greenery. "Not a thing." Revealing the truth might get the boy into hot water. "Why?"

Winona jabbed him with a finger. "Carcajou. Please. Blue Water Woman is right about you."

"Uh-oh." Shakespeare's wife had an uncanny flair for always being right. "What did she say now?"

"That you could not tell a lie if your life depended on it." Winona traced her finger along his jawline. "Your face always gives you away."

"A pox on my face, then, and on me for being as easy to read as an open book. Provided one knows how to make sense of chicken scrawlings scribbled in smeared ink."

Winona gripped his wrist with more strength than was her custom. "You are avoiding my question."

Conceding defeat, Shakespeare disclosed, "He's upset about your visitors. Other than that he won't say."

"Have they insulted him?"

"With other than their presence? Not that I know. But he won't talk to me."

"He'll talk to me," Winona predicted, and hastened in her son's wake. Hiking her buckskin dress, she broke into a run, moving as lithely as a panther, making scant more noise than would the cat she had clashed with on the lakeshore.

Her shoulder pained her, her cuts were sore, but Winona shut them from her mind. She was more concerned about her eldest. Of late he had become unduly irritable, so peckish that on several occasions his anger resulted in sharp exchanges with members of her tribe.

It had nearly brought her to tears. Stalking Coyote had always been the mildest of boys, the most obedient of sons. Now he was as prickly as a wolverine, as volcanic as a geyser.

So drastic a change must have a cause. Winona had tried to pin it down and failed. In her motherly fashion she had sought to cleverly wrest the truth out, but Stalking Coyote foiled her by being unusually closemouthed.

Winona poured on the speed, running with the unconscious grace of an antelope. She vaulted a log, skirted a thicket. In front of her, high weeds shook. "Son?" she called out. "Come here, please."

There was no answer, and Winona suddenly realized the grave mistake she had made. She had plunged into the woods unarmed and alone. Nate would take her to task for being so foolish.

"Stalking Coyote?"

The weeds parted, revealing a dark figure in grimy store-bought clothes. "Afraid not. It's just me," Isaiah said.

"Oh." Winona was surprised. She had moved too swiftly for most men to overtake her, yet somehow Tompkins had gotten ahead. Unless he had been in the woods the whole time, in pursuit of her son himself. But why would Tompkins chase Zach? "Have you seen my boy?"

"I thought I saw him go this way, yes," Isaiah admitted. He did not add that he had been after the brat himself to learn why the youth kept staring at him as if Zach wanted to slice him from navel to neck.

Isaiah had paused to get his bearings when Winona King hollered. Now he tore his eyes from her supple body to prevent his carnal desire from being apparent and said more gruffly than he intended, "I don't know why, but that son of yours doesn't like Rufus and me much."

To deny it would be silly. So Winona didn't. "I am sure it is nothing personal, Mr. Tompkins—"

"Call me Isaiah."

"—Stalking Coyote is just uncomfortable around white men, Mr. Tompkins." Winona deliberately stressed his last name to show their relationship was strictly formal. Nate had taught her all about white customs. What to do and say. What not to do and say. "Several have mistreated him, and I am afraid he bears a grudge."

The lump was back in Isaiah's throat. Coughing, he looked down at the ground and instead wound up gazing at her long, lovely legs, hugged by the soft buckskin. His mouth watered.

Winona did not understand why the New Yorker flushed scarlet. The day was warm, but not *that* warm.

Isaiah coughed more loudly. "Well, he has no right to be spiteful to Rufus and me. We've never done anything to him."

"I am sure—" Winona said, but got no further. For from the weeds behind the white man had materialized a spectral apparition she barely recognized as her own flesh and blood. Features twisted into a mask of hatred, eyes ablaze, Zach crept up close to Isaiah Tompkins and elevated a gleaming butcher knife.

Chapter Ten

The aspens quivered in the breeze as if they shivered from being cold. But the sun was warm on Nate King's bearded face as he prowled among them, the heavy Hawken clutched in his big hands.

Below lay the meadow. The meadow rich with lush grass, staked out by the elk as their very own. Their special grazing ground. Where cows nursed calves. Where, during rutting season, bulls fought fantastic battles for the privilege of siring those calves.

Nate had never shot an elk here before. The meadow was their sanctuary, their home, and he was loath to violate it. But this time he could not afford to spend precious time searching the timber for lone bulls. He had to get back to the cabin as quickly as possible.

Something was bothering him. He could not say exactly what. A vague feeling that had grown during the day. A feeling all was not well. A troubling sense that he *must* return swiftly.

It was all the more unsettling because Nate was not an intuitive person. He wasn't one of those who acted more on feelings than levelheaded thinking.

He tried to chalk it up to needless fretting. Guilt over leaving his loved ones alone with the strangers played heavily on his nerves. That had to be it, he told himself over and over. But a tiny voice deep inside replied, *No, that is not it, and if you do not hurry home you will deeply regret leaving them.*

Perhaps that explained why he blundered. As upset as he was, he did not keep his mind on what he was doing. He did not pay attention to where he was walking, where he placed his feet. When he was close enough to the meadow to see every individual stem of grass, he stepped on a dry twig that cracked like a pistol shot.

Eleven elk were grazing. At the retort, every last one raised its head toward Nate. A bull near the aspens bugled an alarm, and the rest promptly scattered.

Muttering an oath at his own stupidity, Nate barreled on down the slope and out into the open to get a clear shot. Problem was, half the elk had already gained cover and the rest were in full flight. Bringing one down would take skillful shooting.

Nate dropped onto a knee. Wedging the Hawken against his right shoulder, he fixed a hasty bead on a likely target. He held his breath to steady his aim. Lining up the two sights with the elk, he centered them squarely behind the front shoulders. A lung shot was the most reliable. The animal might run on a short distance, but tracking the scarlet spray would be child's play.

His thumb curled back the hammer. His finger curved lightly around the trigger. He pressed his cheek to the stock. Another instant, and he would shoot.

Then the bull stumbled as if it had set a leg into a rut or hole. It staggered to one side, its momentum propelling it headlong to the earth. The great head came up and it bellowed as it struck the ground. From its nostrils spewed crimson. From its side jutted the feathered end of an arrow. Down on its knees, it looked toward the trees.

From out of the aspens strode a giant.

Touch the Clouds had another shaft notched to the sinew string of his ash bow, but he did not raise the bow. Drawing his long knife with the bone handle, he stepped up to the thrashing elk to cut its throat. Without warning the elk lunged, thrusting its antlers at his broad chest.

Touch the Clouds dropped the bow and knife and seized hold of the antlers before they could impale him. Muscles bulging, he held them at bay while the elk grunted and struggled to drive the spikes into him. It surged upward, legs flailing, the desire to live so potent it lent strength to its massive body.

Touch the Clouds dug in his heels and strained his utmost. His people had a saying: Trees are made of wood and bend in the wind; Touch the Clouds is made of rock and does not bend. He proved that now. Sinews rippling, he held the elk down. It snorted and puffed and scrambled at the blood-slick grass but could not stand. Heaving wildly, it wrenched to both sides.

Touch the Clouds changed tactics. Setting himself, he twisted the rack to the right. The bull resisted mightily. Speckled nostrils flared, eyes wide, it fought back with every shred of its being. But Touch the Clouds would not be denied. He continued to slowly twist, slowly turn that thick neck, slowly bend it until the head was at right angles to the body, and still Touch the Clouds twisted. His shoulders swelled, his neck muscles bulged, the veins on his temples were outlined in stark relief.

Animals can sense their doom. This one did. At the very last, the bull went into a frenzy of bellowing and thrashing and pumping legs that would not function.

Touch the Clouds paused, gathering himself, tightening his

granite frame for the final exertion. Then, throwing his full weight and power into the motion, he levered sharply around.

Twenty yards away, Nate King heard the distinct *crack* of vertebrae being shattered. The elk sagged, the huge form limp.

Touch the Clouds let the head fall. From the bull's lips protruded its tongue—a delicacy by Shoshone standards. Picking up his knife, Touch the Clouds sliced off the tip and plopped it into his mouth.

Nate came over, awed. It had been the most incredible exhibition of raw might he had ever witnessed. "The keeper of the past will paint this for posterity."

Split Nose was the oldest Shoshone alive, older even than Spotted Bull, so old that no one living had been alive when he was born. A skilled artist, for more winters than anyone could remember he had taken it on himself to keep a record of important events in the history of his people. He painted the events on buffalo hides kept rolled and stored against wear and tear. Unraveled only on special occasions, the hides were a source of pride to the whole tribe.

Touch the Clouds shrugged. Being remembered for his deeds was unimportant. He chewed on the tongue as Drags the Rope emerged from the aspens.

"Let's get to butchering," Nate proposed, thinking of those who were the whole world to him. "I'll fetch the horses."

"Then you will go," Touch the Clouds said.

"What?"

"Go to your family. Drags the Rope and I will take care of this bull. We will be back tomorrow afternoon at the latest."

Flying to his family on Mercury's flashing wings would not suit Nate as fast enough, but he balked. "It's not fair to the two of you. I should stay."

Drags the Rope motioned. "We have already talked it over. Does a bear leave its cubs alone when wolves are nearby? Go. We do not mind."

Nate's legs pumped toward the aspens. Over his shoulder

he said, "I am grateful. I will always be in your debt."

"You are Shoshone. You are family," said Touch the Clouds.

A warm, fuzzy sensation filled the mountain man as he jogged into the trees. In under three hours, if he pushed the stallion, he would reach the cabin. All would be well.

He could stop fretting.

Shock rooted Winona King in place. Shock that her son would think to stab someone in the *back*. Shock at the mask of unbridled hatred he wore. Shock that the sweet, innocent boy she always envisioned him as could be capable of cold-blooded murder.

"Noooo!" Winona found her vocal chords and sprang forward at the same moment. Arms outflung, she pushed the white man aside just as the knife swept in a tight arc. The glittering steel meant for him now streaked at her.

Isaiah Tompkins was taken aback. Caught flat-footed, he stumbled. He saw the boy, the knife, and comprehended.

Zachary King was livid. He had seen the white man stalking him, and hidden. As much as he wanted to make the man suffer, he would have stayed hidden and let the man blunder about if not for the untimely arrival of his mother. He saw how Tompkins looked at her. And when the white man stepped from the weeds, Zach rose and padded forward. For his mother's own good he was going to end it, then and there.

Rage pounded at him like a hammer on an anvil. Through a swirling mist composed of shimmering reddish pinwheels he saw the New Yorker, and nothing else. It was as if they were the only two people in all Creation. He focused on a spot between the vermin's shoulder blades and hiked his knife for a fatal stroke.

Tensing, Zach drove the tip at Isaiah Tompkins back. Faintly, as if from a great distance, he heard someone yell. Then the greenhorn was in motion, was being shoved out of harm's way, and his own mother was there instead, her face filling his vision and stabbing dismay clear through him.

He was halfway through his swing. He couldn't stop, not in time, not and prevent the blade from shearing into Winona. But he could, and did, shift on the balls of his feet just enough for the knife to miss her by the width of a whisker. He stood quaking with fear at the close shave, then remembered the cause and turned.

Isaiah Tompkins could not believe that someone who was not even old enough to shave had just tried to kill him. He gawked at the glittering steel, stupefied. Anger welled up, animating his limbs. Anger that changed to fear when the boy pivoted toward him and coiled to attack again. Seething blood lust lit the youth's features, reminding Isaiah of some savage beast of prey. "Now, hold on—" he blurted.

Winona sprang between them. Zach took a half-step, starting to go around her, but she shoved a hand against his chest. "Stalking Coyote! What is the meaning of this? What has gotten into you?"

His mother's voice sheared through the reddish mist shrouding Zach's brain. Straightening, he blinked and recovered his wits. "Mother—" he said, his tongue freezing up. How could he tell her the truth?

Horror clutched at Winona's soul. The boy she had given birth to had grown into a bigot, into someone who would kill out of sheer hatred. "How could you? Just because this man is white?"

"What?" Zach said. It took a few moments for the truth to register. His mother believed he had done what he did simply because of the color of the man's skin. How could she think that of him? Hurt, indignant, he opened his mouth to set her straight—and saw Isaiah Tompkins over her shoulder, staring at the back of her body as if she were the rising sun.

A knot formed in Zach's throat and in his stomach. He came

close to pushing his mother out of the way and finishing what he had started. So very, dangerously close.

"I want you to apologize to Mr. Tompkins," Winona demanded. She did not want the New Yorker to think ill of her family, to go back to New York and tell everyone that people who lived on the frontier were rank savages, as so many already assumed.

The words could not get past the knot in Zach's throat, even if he were inclined to obey, which he was not.

"Did you hear me, Stalking Coyote?" Winona said, more sternly than she had addressed her son in her whole life. "I want you to tell him you are sorry."

Zach would rather rip out his tongue.

"Right this instant, if you please."

Uttering a strangled cry of baffled misery, Zach spun and bolted into the trees. Tears moistened his eyes, and he stifled a series of racking sobs. Fleeing blindly, he ran and ran, stopping only when he was too exhausted to go any farther. His emotions in turmoil, he fell to his knees and rocked back and forth, groaning.

Winona started to go after him, then thought better of the notion. He needed time alone to ponder his misdeed. To think about what he had done, how wrong it was. Her cheeks flushing with embarrassment, she faced their guest. "I am afraid I must do the apologizing, Mr. Tompkins. Please forgive him. He can be a bit spirited at times, just like any boy."

"Spirited?" Isaiah said, and laughed coldly. "Playing pranks is spirited. Sneaking liquor when the parents are away is spirited. Doing things behind their backs is spirited. But what your son just tried to do was rank *murder*. If you hadn't intervened, your son would have buried that knife in my back. You know he would have. So don't stand there and tell me it was something any boy would do."

Winona could feel her cheeks grow a darker shade of red. She felt so awkward, so at a loss. "What you say is true. I assure you, though, it will not happen again. My husband and I will take steps to guarantee your safety for the remainder of your stay."

It was then, like a bolt out of the blue, that a bright burst of inspiration hit Isaiah. An idea so fantastic, so titillating, so devious, he was amazed at his own brilliance. "I don't know . . ." he stalled, buying time to form his thoughts.

Winona gazed into the undergrowth, wishing she had gone after Zach. Maybe she had made a mistake in not talking to him, in getting him to explain.

"Your husband will be gone for a day or two, I understand," Isaiah said. "Are you going to watch over me every minute of every hour until he returns?"

"Well, I—"

Isaiah did not let her finish. "Of course you can't. Sooner or later that boy will get his chance. And then what? I bear him no malice, Winona. I don't want to hurt him. I would rather he kill me than lift a finger against someone his age." Inwardly, Isaiah chuckled at his supposedly noble sentiments.

Winona was torn. Tompkins had a point. She couldn't be at his side every minute. She could, though, ask Shakespeare to help, and she said so.

Isaiah had to think fast. "I'm grateful, but I don't want to impose any more than I already have. Besides, what if your son tries to shoot me from ambush? McNair might take the ball or arrow meant for me."

Zach would never! Winona was going to respond, but she stilled her tongue. After what he had just done, maybe he would. Maybe she did not know her son as well as she had always taken for granted she did.

"I have a better idea," Isaiah quickly went on, taking advantage of her sorrow and confusion. "My friend and I are eager to head on home. All we would need are three or four horses and a sack of food. And some ammunition."

Winona pursed her lips. The horses could be spared. Nate

had plenty of ammunition. And she had enough jerked venison on hand to last the greenhorns a couple of weeks if they rationed it wisely.

"We could leave first thing in the morning," Isaiah suggested. "We'd be out of your hair. Safe from your son."

The more Winona considered it, the more she liked the idea. Nate had been planning to send them on their way soon, anyway. "I could help you," she offered.

Pure delight coursed through Isaiah. He had her right where he wanted her. "There are a couple of conditions, though."

"Conditions?"

"Yes. It would be best if no one else knew. Not even McNair. If word somehow leaked to Zachary, he might take it into his head to ambush us on our way out."

"Yes, he just might," Winona had to concede.

"One other thing," Isaiah said, and paused. Everything depended on how persuasive he could now be. "Rufus and I aren't woodsmen. We don't know how to track. Or to follow a trail very well. We're rather helpless in that regard. So I was wondering . . ." He lowered his voice. "I was wondering if you'd consent to guide us down to the prairie. I'm worried about straying off the trail and winding up God-knows-where."

Winona mulled the request.

"I know it's silly. Two grown men getting lost in broad daylight. But that trail twists and turns a lot, and the going is steep in spots. I'm sorry we're so helpless. If you'd consent to lead us, I'm sure we wouldn't have a problem."

His humility touched her. And yes, Winona had known other whites whose wilderness savvy was, to put it mildly, downright pathetic.

"We'd be greatly in your debt," Isaiah said. Forgetting himself, he impulsively clasped her hand. "Please. I don't want your son to go through life with the burden of my death on his conscience."

Winona pulled her hand free. His own had been cold and clammy, like the scales of a fish. She overlooked his forwardness, blaming it on his anxiety.

"Please," Isaiah begged one last time.

"Very well."

Triumph made Isaiah want to whoop for joy. Instead, he beamed and gushed, "Thank you, thank you, thank you. I'll break the good news to Rufus. We'll be ready to go at the crack of dawn."

"No, before it," Winona said. "We must leave while it is still dark. I will wake you at the proper time, and have everything in readiness. We will sneak off with no one being the wiser."

"You're an angel, Winona."

"It is Mrs. King to you," Winona reminded him.

"Oh. I'm sorry. Of course. It's just that I'm so excited at the prospect of going back, I can hardly contain myself." Isaiah envisioned the two of them entwined on a grassy glade, and had to avert his face once again so she wouldn't notice his hunger.

Winona misconstrued. Thinking he was overcome with joy, she politely put a hand on his shoulder. "Trust me, Mr. Tompkins. I will lead you safely to the prairie. Before you know it, you will be back with your family and friends."

"I can hardly wait."

Smiling, Winona departed. Once the white men were gone, she would sit down with Stalking Coyote. Have a long mother-to-son talk. Save him from himself. All would be well again. As it had been before the white men came, only better.

Isaiah watched the Shoshone woman leave, his loins twitching at the seductive sway to her hips. God, it had been so long since he had a woman. Since he savored the taste of a luscious female. He had almost forgotten how sweetly delirious it made him. He had been a fool to think he could go without.

Chuckling at his clever deceit, Isaiah hefted his rifle and

trudged after her. A rustling sound to his right reminded him of the sole hitch to his scheme. Whirling, he trained the muzzle on the spot. No one appeared, so after a minute he hurried in a roundabout route to the lean-to. He didn't want anyone to see him anywhere near Winona King. No one must suspect what he was up to. That included his best friend.

Rufus Stern squatted beside a small fire he had kindled to boil coffee graciously given to them by their host. He jumped when a shadow fell across the interior, automatically reaching for his rifle. "Oh! It's you!"

"Miss me?"

"Where the hell have you been? I've been on pins and needles."

"I went for a stroll. Needed to stretch my legs," Isaiah lied, sinking down. "What's wrong with that? You traipsed around earlier, if you'll recall, and I didn't raise a fuss."

"I just worried, is all." Rufus didn't mention his worry was for Winona King. As much as he liked Isaiah, he had to be honest. Where women were concerned, Isaiah was a regular fanatic. Any beautiful woman who caught his eye was ripe for conquest.

A particular instance came to mind. A couple of years before they had been ambling along a city street when Isaiah spotted a ravishing redhead in a passing carriage. He had chased the carriage for four blocks, seeking to learn the woman's identity.

At the time Rufus had thought it comical. There was his silly friend, frantically trying to keep pace while declaring his devotion to a woman he had never met. But damned if she didn't order the driver to stop so she could give Isaiah a slip of paper bearing her name and address. As it turned out, she was married. Yet that did not keep her from dallying.

Rufus hadn't approved. New York swarmed with eligible single women, many as lovely as fabled Cleopatra. Married ones should be left alone. Isaiah had laughed when he made his· opinion known, and flatly told Rufus that "married wenches add thrill to the chase, zest to the lovemaking. As far as I'm concerned, any woman is fair game, wed or not."

And now Isaiah had his eyes set on their host's wife. Rufus had seen her emerge from the forest a short while ago. "Were you off with Mrs. King, by any chance? What were the two of you doing?"

"I have no idea where she was. I'll thank you to cease thinking ill of me. Honestly, Rufus. You act as if I'm the worst lecher who ever lived."

Rufus grew defensive. "I never said that!" he complained. And let it drop. His fears were probably groundless. Even Isaiah had limits. To change the subject, he asked, "Did you see anything of the King boy?"

"Nary a hair," Isaiah added to his string of deceptions. It would be nice if he knew where the youth had gotten to, though. Just so he could keep an eye on the firebrand. Zach was the one person who might thwart him.

At that exact second, a quarter of a mile to the southwest, the object of the New Yorker's interest was hunched over, beating the earth with his fists, venting his fury the only way he could think to do so.

Zach was madder than he had ever been. If Isaiah Tompkins had appeared at that moment, Zach would have torn the man apart with his bare hands.

He pounded the ground again and again, pounded until his hands ached and his knuckles were raw. Seething in torment, he slumped forward, resting his forehead on the grass. A groan escaped him.

What was he to do? Going back to the cabin would reap a tongue-lashing from his mother. She simply did not understand. And he could not bring himself to come right out and say that Tompkins had been undressing her with his eyes. She was his *mother*.

Some things were never discussed in the King household. Intimate relations was one of them. His father had taken him aside when he was eleven and imparted the information he would one day need to "carry on the King line." But that was the extent of it.

Gentlemen did not talk about such things in front of ladies. His pa had ingrained the teaching into his skull from early childhood. Women were to be treated with respect. Always. Without exception.

His time spent among the Shoshones reinforced the teaching. Some tribes allowed their women to mix freely with whites, to sell their bodies for baubles. The Shoshones frowned on the practice. Womanhood was held in high esteem. Not quite as strictly as among the Cheyennes, who were known to compel their maidens to wear leather chastity belts. But exalted nonetheless.

It was unthinkable, what Isaiah Tompkins was doing. Zach knew his father would throttle the man within an inch of his life. He contemplated sneaking back, saddling his horse, and going to find his pa. He had a fair idea of where the hunters had gone. But that might take the better part of a day—leaving his mother with no one to protect her other than Shakespeare and old Spotted Bull.

Zach thought of telling his uncle. They had always been close. Yet knowing Shakespeare as he did, Zach suspected the mountain man would "go have a little talk" with the New Yorker rather than do what really needed doing.

No, Zach was strictly on his own. The responsibility for safeguarding his ma was his and his alone. He would stay aloof but close by, ready to leap to her defense.

Holding his knife aloft so the blade shone with mirrored sunlight, Zach King solemnly, silently vowed to take the white man's life if Isaiah Tompkins overstepped the bounds of decency. His rage had subsided. In its place a chilling resolve spread. He would never let down his guard. For as sure as he lived and breathed, the white man was going to reveal his vile nature, and when that happened, Zach would be there.

He could always use another scalp.

Chapter Eleven

The mishap took place an hour after Nate King left Touch the Clouds and Drags the Rope at the high country meadow.

In his eagerness to get back to the cabin, in his anxiety over his family, Nate had been spurring the black stallion at a reckless pace. The big horse was showing signs of fatigue, and by rights Nate should have stopped for a while to let it rest. The forested slopes were thick with impassable deadfalls and crisscrossed by deep ruts and defiles worn by erosion.

No mountaineer or Indian with a lick of common sense would have done what Nate was doing. Part of him kept saying *Slow down!* He was fully aware of the great risk he was taking.

Nate counted on luck, and Providence, to safeguard him. Having survived countless scrapes and close shaves over the years, he felt confident the Almighty would watch over him now.

It didn't help, though, that the sun had dipped behind a high jagged peak to the west, plunging the treacherous slope into premature twilight. Nor did it help that the high firs tended to blot out much of the remaining light.

Nate was vigilant every second. He constantly had to avoid obstacles. A log here, boulders there, elsewhere a rift or an extremely dense thicket.

Lesser horsemen would have been too intimidated to hold to the pace he did. Only someone completely at home in the saddle, someone who had spent the greater portion of their adult life with their feet in stirrups, could fly down that slope as he did.

Ironic, since at one time Nate had harbored a secret fear of horses. When he was small, just a sprout, his father had sent him to a relative's farm in upstate New York for a week. "Just for the experience," his father had said.

The farmer had been a boisterous sort, loud and rough but as sincere as a parson. Nate had been in awe, both of him and the many animals that called the farm home. Cows, chickens, roosters, hogs, goats, geese, turkeys, pigeons, Nate encountered them all.

The cows amazed him. How they could convert grass into milk was a mystery too incredible to fathom. The farmer had taught him how to squeeze the teats, and he had delighted in filling a pail even though much of the milk wound up everywhere except in the bucket.

One of his jobs was to collect eggs every morning. He learned that some chickens did not want their eggs taken, and his hands were pecked sore.

The hogs disgusted him. All they did was eat and sleep and wallow in revolting filth. He had decided never to eat ham again, but the taste proved too irresistible.

Then there were the draft horses. Enormous, thick-limbed animals, they'd scared Nate half to death. To his childish mind, they were like creatures out of deepest Africa. Giants that could crush him with a single misstep. He'd helped harness them, terrified every second that one would turn and bite an arm off.

Later, Nate had ridden a pony. A small, cute little pony he had petted and stroked before being lifted on, bareback. His father's cousin had said not to worry, that the pony was the "tamest animal ever born." Nate had giggled while riding in a small circle, proud of himself. Wishing his father could see.

Then a bee buzzed the pony's head. The next thing, Nate was being bounced wildly, every bone jarred, and the farmer was hollering for him to hold on tight. It had been easy for the man to say, but there had been precious little to grab. The reins were no use. The mane was short and stringy. Nate had tried to wrap his arms around the neck, but he was bucked off before he could get a grip.

Miraculously, he'd been spared serious harm. The farmer had laughed and clapped him on the back, joking that he'd looked like a drunk crow as he flew through the air. Nate failed to see the humor. And for many years his stomach had balled into a knot whenever he was near a horse.

Now those childhood memories washed over him. Nate relived again that awful moment when the bee swooped in close to the pony's face. He could feel himself being thrown, feel the air rush past his face.

Almost simultaneously, the big black stumbled on a steep, gravel-strewn incline.

Nate clutched at the saddle horn and pressed his legs against its sides. The stallion dipped violently, pitching him forward. He was flung over its neck. His Hawken went flying. Tucking, he hit on his shoulder and rolled, relieved he had escaped unscathed and praying the stallion had done the same.

He tumbled, unable to arrest his descent. A glancing blow to the side lanced him with pain. Then he seemed to be floating—or, rather, falling through empty space. The next impact was enough to stun him.

Dazed, Nate grunted and slowly sat up. He had lost his hat

and one of his pistols. His right shoulder ached terribly. It was much darker, and he discovered why when he craned his neck.

The fall had pitched him into a cleft. A narrow defile, two feet wide, maybe eight feet long, the walls a good ten to twelve feet in height. Sheer walls, as smooth as glass. Frowning, Nate braced his back against a side and straightened. His left ankle protested.

Rising to his full height, Nate stretched an arm as high as he could. His fingers were well shy of the rim. Seeking handholds and finding none, he attempted to climb anyway, digging his fingers into the hard-packed earth. Only, it wasn't as hard-packed as he assumed. It came apart, dissolved in his grip, raining dirt and dust and denying him freedom.

"Son of a—" Nate fumed.

The other side was no better. Nate clawed and scratched, showering more debris to the bottom, gouging furrows in the walls.

He was trapped.

It was every mountain man's worst nightmare made real. No one was around to lend a hand. Shouting would be a waste of energy. Brute strength would not suffice. He must rely on his wits.

Resisting the prick of panic, Nate bent his knees as far as they would bend. Girding himself, he hurtled upward, jumping high—but not high enough. In a shower of loose dirt and pebbles, he fell back.

I have to think! Nate told himself. There had to be a way out. There just had to be. Sidling to the left, he roved the length of the ravine. He found no gaps, no breaks, nothing he could capitalize on.

Nate swallowed hard. He recollected the time Shakespeare and he had come on a skeleton along a remote creek, the wrist bones still caught in the grip of a rusty saw-toothed beaver trap. As best they could reconstruct what had happened, the man had been setting the trap and somehow triggered it on his own arm. Shakespeare guessed a vein or artery had been severed. Weakening fast from loss of blood, the man had been unable to free himself. And there had been no one around to save him.

Scrape marks on the bone hinted at the despair the poor trapper had felt. With his strength waning, he had torn and tugged at the unrelenting steel. Death, Shakespeare reckoned, had been a good long while in coming. Nate had shuddered as they rode away after giving the bones a decent burial.

The secret fear of practically every frontiersman was to die alone, in misery, unmourned, forlorn—it was the ultimate horror.

Lending urgency to Nate's predicament was his growing sense that something was wrong at home. He must get there, quickly. Again he clawed at the side, gaining brief purchase and rising maybe half a foot. It wasn't enough. Gravity pulled him back down. Frustrated, mad, he smashed a fist against the opposite wall.

A noise above drew his gaze. The stallion was moving around. He heard the saddle creak, the plod of hooves. "Here, big fella!" he called, but the horse did not heed. It didn't matter. The stallion couldn't throw him a rope or haul him out. He was totally on his own. "There has to be a way," he declared.

Nate roved the cleft twice more, seeking footholds. There were none. Overhead, what little light existed slowly faded. It was so dark at the bottom that he could barely see his hand when he held it at arm's length.

Worry gnawed at his innards like a wolf gnawing a bone. Nate drew his knife and commenced digging a hole at shoulder height. When it was deep enough, he stretched up onto his toes and dug another. Then, replacing the knife, he inserted his left hand in the lowest, his right in the highest, and levered himself upward.

It should have worked. It should have propelled him high

enough to make a grab for the top. But no sooner did he apply pressure than both holes gave way, the dirt crumbling like so much rotted wood, crumbling to pieces and dumping him back down.

Nate bit his lower lip so as not to swear a blue streak. He must keep his head. He would get out of there! He would! It was just a question of time.

The cleft grew steadily darker.

Rufus Stern was awake but had no idea what had awakened him. Inky pitch clung to his eyes. He blinked but could see no better. Annoyed that he had been roused from a deep sleep so early, he started to roll back over when a hand gripped his shoulders.

"Rise and shine, layabout."

"What?" Rufus squinted and distinguished a silhouette. "Isaiah? What are you doing up this soon? You, of all people. Let me sleep, will you?"

"Get ready."

"Quit babbling and get some more rest." Rufus closed his eyes and smacked his lips. He would deal with the idiot later.

"We're leaving."

"What?" Rufus said sleepily. He couldn't have heard what he thought he heard. They weren't going to depart until after Nate returned. Another two days, at least, according to McNair. Plenty of opportunity for him to catch up on his sleep and recuperate from their ordeal.

"We're leaving," Isaiah repeated.

"Quit it. You're not funny."

Isaiah smacked Stern on the chest. "You dunderhead! Gather up your stuff. Unless you'd rather be left behind." A minute before, Winona had shaken him awake and pressed a finger to his mouth to warn him to keep silent. After whispering instructions, she had melted away without a sound.

It struck Rufus that his childhood chum was serious. "What?"

"Do I have to spell it out for you? We're going. Mounts and pack animals are waiting for us in the pines. So get your lazy backside out of those blankets and collect your gear. Me, I'm not staying a second longer than I have to."

"What?" Astounded, Rufus sat up.

"Quit saying that. You sound like a silly parrot." Isaiah had made sure his rifle was loaded and his meager possessions in order the evening before. He had not forewarned Rufus, since his friend was bound to squawk.

Shaking himself, suddenly chill to the marrow, Rufus stared at the quiet cabin and the still tepees, vague masses in the night. "Are you insane? You're stealing horses from the Kings? What do you think Nate will do when he finds out?"

"What do you take me for? One of them is helping us. Now, pull on your boots and let's go."

Befuddled, Rufus blindly did as Isaiah requested. Tugging on his battered footwear, he claimed his leather pouch and his long gun. His legs were unsteady as he rose, his blood as sluggish as molasses. Frozen molasses. "Where to?"

"Follow me."

Rufus took a step and nearly tripped over something on the ground. Cautiously skirting it, he bumped his head on the top of the lean-to. "Ouch," he blurted, and rubbed his scalp as he stumbled into the open.

"Damn it! Quit acting the fool!"

Clawed fingers clamped onto Rufus's arm and he was roughly hauled to the left, into the benighted woods that buffered the homestead. Grass clung to his feet. Roots tried to snag his legs. Groping in stark fear, he thrust his other arm out to ward off branches that might gouge his eyes and face.

"Hurry up!" Isaiah hissed. The fool was making enough racket to raise the dead. And Indians and mountain men were notoriously light sleepers. He would not tolerate any interference, not now, not when he was so close. Should anyone presume to intervene, he was fully prepared to shoot them dead.

Rufus winced when a limb scraped his cheek. "Can't we go a little slower?" he protested, and was dragged *faster*. He did not see why they were rushing so. Prudence called for taking it nice and slow.

Isaiah eased counting how many steps he took. At twenty, he abruptly stopped and looked around. This should be it. But there was no sign of the vision of loveliness or the horses. Had he erred? Had he strayed instead of bearing due east? Taking a chance, he whispered loudly, "Where are you?"

"I'm right here," Rufus answered, and chuckled. "You've got my arm, remember?"

Isaiah was beginning to wonder why he had put up with Stern for so many years, why he had saddled himself with a moron for a boon companion. "Not you," he snarled, and stiffened as an hourglass shape materialized.

"This way," Winona said. It had taken a heap of doing, as her husband would say, but she had packed parfleches with everything they would need and prepared the horses without anyone catching on. A note on the table asked Shakespeare to take care of Evelyn until she got back, which shouldn't be later than noon the next day.

"Winona?" Rufus said as he was led deeper into the vegetation. What was she doing there? Oh, God! Isaiah had mentioned someone was helping them. The unthinkable must be happening! Winona King and Isaiah were running off together! Stealing away in the dead of predawn!

"Wait," Rufus said, wanting to talk, but Isaiah yanked so hard he almost lost his footing. They should discuss it. Isaiah must be made to understand the gravity of his mistake. Nate King would hunt them to the ends of the earth, if that was what it took to get his wife back.

Isaiah wasn't waiting for anyone or anything. Jaw muscles clenched, he hustled Rufus along. From out of the stygian veil loomed the horses. Winona was mounting one. Isaiah shoved Rufus at another, then forked a sorrel.

"We will walk them until we reach the lake," Winona directed. That should be long enough. The soft soil along the shore would muffle the hoofbeats. Once they were on the other side they could ride like the wind.

Rufus reluctantly climbed on. He did not want to go, but neither did he care to be left behind. Nate might blame him in some respect. Or the Shoshones might hold him to account. And that giant terrified him. The previous night he'd had an awful dream in which Touch the Clouds tied him to a spit and roasted him over a roaring fire.

Against his better judgment, Rufus trailed the packhorses as Winona threaded through the trees. Twice he came close to being knocked off by low branches she artfully avoided. She must have eyes like a cat, he mused. The woman was wonderfully competent, more so than most men.

Isaiah stayed close to Winona's mare just to catch an occasional whiff of the minty fragrance she favored. An herbal concoction, no doubt, tantalizing just the same. Presently, they were in the open, a brisk wind from the lake stirring his hair. He could see her now, her beautiful profile, her ripe body. As soon as she escorted them safely to the prairie, that body would be his to savor as he desired. And if Rufus objected, well—Isaiah unconsciously fingered his rifle's trigger.

Isaiah had no qualms about the course he had chosen. He had always been one to put his own interests and desires ahead of others'. Why shouldn't he? Everyone else did it—with a few pathetic exceptions like Rufus, yacks who were sheep in human guise. Maybe that was why he had tolerated Rufus for so long. Stern was like a little lost puppy who needed a master to lead him around on a tight leash.

Isaiah glanced at his friend, debating whether to reveal the truth about Rufus's beloved Agnes. The simpleton doted on her, believed she was God's gift to womanhood. Isaiah knew better. He was intimately familiar with every curve of her rather plump figure; he knew the contours of her body better than the man who was pledged to marry her. Isaiah laughed bitterly.

"Is something wrong?" Winona asked. She attributed the strange mirth to bad nerves. People did peculiar things when they were afraid.

"No," Isaiah answered, and laughed again, gaily. Everything was going right for once. Soon they would cross the valley and start their descent. McNair or the old Indian might try to overtake them, but he wasn't worried. Neither would anticipate a lead ball between the eyes.

Rufus was petrified. Continually glancing over a shoulder, he wore his neck sore before they rounded the south shore. It wouldn't be long before someone showed up. Which spelled trouble. Trouble he wanted no part of.

Rufus didn't think it fair for Isaiah to draw him into the brewing conflict. *He* had no interest in the Shoshone. Sweet Agnes Weatherby was the only woman for him, the only one he'd ever wanted, the only one he would ever need. The Good Lord had blessed their union with perfect love, a love as pure as freshly minted gold, as unshakable as the foundations of the earth itself.

A pink tinge to the eastern horizon goaded Winona to greater speed. So long as they were through the gap that linked the valley to the outside world before the sun came up, they would be fine. She scanned the trees without cease, glad they had gotten as far as they had without incident.

Her thoughts strayed to her husband. Winona hoped the hunt had gone well, that before another day had gone by she would hold him in her arms and lavish hot kisses on his lips and face. What was he doing at that exact instant? she wondered. Still sound asleep? Doubtful, since he had always been up before the crack of dawn.

The important thing was that Nate was safe, with two of

his most trusted friends. She couldn't conceive of any harm befalling him, not with Touch the Clouds and Drags the Rope at his side.

At least she had one less worry.

Nate King wiped his sweaty brow with a dirty sleeve and squinted at the rectangle of slightly lighter darkness above. So close, yet so far. So elusive. All night long he had tried to escape the damnable trench, and all he had to show for it were filthy buckskins, more bruises and scrapes than he could shake a stick at, and a partially buckled wall that had filled the cleft as high as his ankles.

Fatigue was taking its toll. Nate was so tired, he couldn't concentrate. Sagging, he mulled his next move. What was there left to do when he had tried everything he could think of? Digging handholds had failed. Propping his arms and feet against the two walls and shimmying higher had been futile. Scrambling out at either end had proved a waste of energy. One idea after another, all rank failures.

He did not know exactly what time it was, but his internal clock hinted daylight was not far off.

Nate was at the end of his rope. Food and rest would invigorate him, but he might as well wish upon a star. Tilting his head back, he hunkered to think. The feeling of being hemmed had grown unbearable. He had to remind himself that the walls were not going to topple, that he wasn't on the verge of being buried alive.

Scooping up a handful of dirt, he randomly dropped it near his left moccasin. The sprinkles raised pale puffs of dust. Deep in thought, he dropped another handful on top of the first. Then a third, and a fourth. Shifting to survey the far end, he placed his hand on the pile and felt how high it had grown.

High? Nate slowly unfurled and palmed his butcher knife. Moving to a point where the earth was especially dry and loose, he tore into it as if he intended to bore clear to China.

With every sweep of his blade more dirt cascaded around his feet. It rose over his toes, his ankles, and climbed up his pants legs.

Until a few moments before Nate had been wary of causing a total collapse. Now he no longer cared. He would escape or he would die in the attempt.

Nate's arm flew. Dust swirled thick, choking his nostrils, making him cough. Covering his mouth and nose with his other hand, he embedded the knife again and again and again. More and more earth was dislodged. The flow became a torrent. The level rose halfway to his knees and still he dug, dug, dug, even while scrambling higher on the ever-rising pile.

It was a long shot at best. Yet it was his only hope of escape before weakness and hunger brought him low.

Somewhere, the stallion nickered. Nate never slackened his pace. When his right arm grew tired, he switched the knife to his left. Swing, twist, tug. Swing, twist, tug. The same movement repeated endlessly. Repeated until his shoulders throbbed. Repeated until his arms were leaden. Repeated until he did not think he could lift the knife anymore.

But lift it he did. Mechanically forcing his body to obey, Nate dug a cavity wide enough and high enough for Evelyn to stand in. It wasn't enough. The dirt was as high as his knees. It had to be a lot higher. Spearing the knife at the right edge, he gouged deep and jerked. When the blade came away, so did a gigantic portion of the wall.

Nate flung both forearms in front of his face as a tidal wave slammed into him. An enormous weight smashed into his chest, ramming him against the other side, pinning him fast. He swatted and kicked and thrashed, but it was like trying to move through rapidly hardening quicksand.

Gradually the flow dwindled. Nate was up to his arms in dirt, unable to move his legs or body. He had held on to the knife, but it would take forever to dig himself out. Wrenching to the right and the left, he fought to gain enough freedom of movement to clamber to safety. But he was encased in an earthen cocoon. His sinews were useless. Now he was worse off than before.

Exhaustion took its toll. Nate's chin slumped. His skin itched terribly and he was caked with perspiration. Beads of it trickled down his ears, across his neck. A low *thump* reminded him he wasn't alone.

Fifteen feet away grazed the stallion. Reins dangling, it cropped sweet grass, its tail swishing although no flies were abroad to pester it. Nate beckoned and urged, "Over here, Nightwind. Come to me."

The horse would rather eat.

"Come," Nate said gently. Setting down the knife, he held out both hands. "Please."

A flip of its tail was like a slap in the face. "Now!" Nate snapped, raising his voice, forgetting what was at stake. Upsetting it, driving it off, would seal his fate. Instantly reverting to a calm, friendly tone, he said, "Please, boy. Walk on over here and bend your head so I can grab the bridle. Come on, Nightwind. You can do it. I know you can."

The stallion did not budge.

Inspiration prompted Nate to cup his right hand and extend it farther. "How would you like some sugar, Nightwind? Your favorite." He wagged his hand as he often did when offering a real treat. "All yours. What do you say?" At last the stallion lifted its head and looked at him. "Sugar. Remember?" Smacking his lips, he pretended to be eating some. Nightwind whinnied softly.

Nate patiently waited, his life hanging in the balance.

Chapter Twelve

A blazing sun crowned the sky, bathing the foothills in its rosy glow, spreading welcome warmth and stirring myriad wild creatures to life. The sunrise was spectacular, but Isaiah Tompkins did not notice. His sole interest was a different example of rare beauty.

From the moment Isaiah could see Winona clearly, he didn't take his gaze off her. He drank in the sight of her raven tresses and her supple figure much as a parched desert wanderer would drink in the sight of an oasis. God, he *wanted* her. He wanted to touch her, feel her, rove his hands and lips all over her. Just thinking about the act spread tingly warmth throughout his whole body.

Rufus Stern noticed, and his anxiety mounted. He had seen that look on his friend many times before, always right before Isaiah indulged in one of his notorious ''conquests.'' Rufus didn't like it one bit. The Kings had treated them decently. This was not how Nate and Winona should be repaid for their kindness.

Isaiah was acting like a crazy man. Like someone gone mad with unchecked passion. Rufus had always known his friend was unduly fond of the opposite sex. But *this* was carrying it to an extreme no sane man ever would.

Rufus conjured an image of his darling Agnes floating before his eyes, and how he would feel if someone presumed to trifle with her. Why, he would be outraged. He wasn't by nature a violent man, but he would gladly pound the offender to a pulp.

Winona was intent on navigating the trail, on leading the packhorses swiftly lower. Eager to get the chore over with and return to her family, she did not pay much attention to the white men. Not until they were a mile below the gap did she rein up on a grassy shelf to give the animals a brief breather. "We'll rest here a bit," she said, facing the greenhorns.

Rufus was staring at Isaiah in apparent annoyance. Isaiah was staring at her. Winona looked into his eyes—and shock ripped through her. The hungry gleam was unmistakable. She had seen it too many times on other men to mistake it for anything other than what it was. But never this intense.

Quickly turning, Winona acted as if she hadn't noticed. Dismounting, she walked to the edge of the shelf to scout the land below—and to think. For now that she reflected on the few times she had been in Isaiah Tompkins's company, she realized there had been subtle clues all along about how he felt toward her.

How could she have been so blind? Why hadn't she seen them sooner? Winona had been much more sensitive to such attention when she was younger. Being married had made her complacent. She took it for granted other men would let her be.

Winona wasn't unduly worried. She had her rifle and two pistols and a knife. Should Tompkins be brash enough to insult her, she would put him in his place readily enough. Then she heard the metallic click of a gun hammer being pulled back.

"Drop your weapons. All of them. And put your hands in the air."

Winona pivoted and froze. The muzzle of Tompkins's rifle was fixed on her midsection. His finger was on the trigger. "Consider what you are doing."

"I have thought about it. It's all I've thought about since I met you." Isaiah licked his dry lips. He'd seen the flash of recognition when she glanced at him. Regrettable, since it forced his hand, but it couldn't be helped. "Do as I told you."

"You won't shoot me," Winona blustered. "You want me alive. You want me whole."

"Yes, I want you," Isaiah admitted, "but a hurt leg won't hamper us too much." He pointed the barrel at her left thigh. "Last warning."

Winona gauged her chances of leaping aside and firing before he could shoot her. At that close range they were slim. Lowering the Hawken, she gingerly drew both pistols and let them fall at her feet. The same with her long knife.

"Excellent," Isaiah commented. His throat was raw, his body hot. Below his belt was a bulge that hurt. His temples began to pound as he advanced a step, openly ogling the swell of her bosom. At that second in time he wanted her more than he had ever wanted any woman. "We're going into the trees," he announced.

"You're not going anywhere."

Isaiah did not turn his head. There was no need. He knew Rufus had trained a gun on him. "So. The mouse squeaks. Stay out of this. It's none of your affair."

"Like hell it isn't!" Rufus Stern declared. His mind was made up. Just as he would not allow anyone to violate Agnes, he could not sit idly by while his friend did the same to this decent woman, either. Rape was a hideous act. Quaking with indignation, he leaned forward. "I mean it, Isaiah! You set down that rifle this minute and you step away from her, or so help me God I'll blow a hole in you!"

Isaiah believed it. Slowly rotating, careful to keep Winona covered, he forced a grin and said, "I should have known you wouldn't have the stomach for this. For old times' sake, Rufe, keep going. I'll catch up directly."

"No. It's wrong. It's vile. I won't let you." Rufus looked at Winona. "I'm sorry, Mrs. King. I truly am. I should have done something sooner."

"You have done fine," Winona said, uncomfortably conscious of the muzzle still pointed at her. She knew that if she bent to grab one of her weapons, Tompkins would shoot. "Disarm him, and we will go back. No harm will come to you. I give you my word."

Rufus nodded. "You heard the lady, Isaiah."

That Isaiah had. The moment of decision was upon him. A distraction was called for, and he had just the thing. "All right, Rufus. You win. I appreciate how you're trying to save me from myself." His grin widened. "It's only fair I return the favor."

"How so?"

"Agnes. Your dearest Agnes."

Straightening, Rufus demanded, "What about her?"

"Remember that time a whole bunch of us went to New Jersey? To the shore? We rented cabins for the weekend and spent the days lying in the sun and swimming, our nights strolling along the beach and roasting corn over a fire?"

Sure, Rufus remembered. There had been six guys and seven girls. Agnes's own mother had served as chaperon, but her rheumatism had kept her pretty much confined to her cabin. "It was one of the best weekends I ever had."

"Remember the evening Agnes disappeared for over an hour? How worried her mother was? How worried you were?"

How could Rufus ever forget? Everyone searched and searched, all except Isaiah, who had gone to town. Agnes turned up safe later on, much to his relief, saying she had taken a long walk, lain down, and fallen asleep. The incoming tide had awakened her. They had shared a laugh over the wet sand that clung to the back of her dress, and her disheveled hair. "What about it?" he asked uneasily.

"Did you truly believe she had been asleep all that time?" Isaiah snickered.

The blood drained from Rufus's face. "No. Agnes wouldn't have."

"Come, now. Surely you suspected? And that was just the first time."

Rufus had been suspicious, but he had chalked it up to an overly jealous nature. Now he saw her periodic absences in a whole new light. Sweet Agnes. *His* Agnes. She had betrayed his trust, despoiled their devotion. A groan fluttered from deep within him, and he bowed his head in despair. "Oh, my love, my love," he said forlornly.

"Oh, you dolt, you dolt," Isaiah mimicked, and shot his best friend in the chest. Rufus was lifted clear of the saddle, flung brutally to the ground, and lay with glazing eyes wide in astonishment.

Surprise slowed Winona a second too long. She lunged for a pistol, but Isaiah was already springing. They collided, grappled. The stock of his rifle drove into her stomach, doubling her in half. Tottering backward, she felt her right foot slide over the edge.

Isaiah clutched at her shoulder. In desperation Winona grabbed his wrist. Neither move was sufficient to keep her from going over the side. Down she went, pulling him after her. A bush snared her legs and she cartwheeled, breaking his hold. End over end she fell, losing all sense of up and down, of where the sky and ground should be.

The slope seemed to go on forever. Finally Winona slid to a lurching halt. Covered by welts, scrapes, and bruises, she stiffly rose onto her elbows. If she could get to her feet and up the slope to her guns before the white man recovered, she would—

A muttered curse sounded in her ear. A hand wound into her hair and jerked her to her knees.

"I nearly broke my neck thanks to you."

Winona caught a slap full across the face. Rocked backward, she covered her stinging cheek and glared at the lecher. Evidently, he had lost his rifle in the fall.

"I'll take the fight out of you." Isaiah sneered. "Then we can enjoy ourselves in earnest."

Like an enraged bobcat, Winona came up off the ground in a blur, her nails searing his neck as her other hand sought the knife at his hip.

Isaiah backpedaled in alarm. He was accustomed to tame women. To docile females who tittered coyly and meekly did whatever he wished. The only time a woman had ever resisted his advances had been when a matron used her knee where it would hurt the most and then left him lying in the dust. Which had been just as well. She hadn't really been his type.

No one had ever fought back as furiously as Winona King. Isaiah was momentarily bewildered. He warded off another raking blow while grabbing for his knife hilt. Like someone possessed, she lit into him with a vengeance, tearing open his chin, then going for his eyes. It was all he could do to keep from being blinded.

Anger flared. Resentment that the squaw would not submit—that she dared to resist her better. Balling a fist, Isaiah rammed it into her ribs. "Damn you, you red bitch!" he hissed.

Acute agony spiked through Winona. Gasping for breath, she teetered. As quick and strong as she was, she was no match for Tompkins in a brute clash. She must flee. Living was more important than venting her spite. Whirling, she ran toward a patch of trees, but she had not taken more than four bounds when arms wrapped around her shins and she was brought crashing down.

"No, you don't," Isaiah huffed.

Winona was flipped over, her chest straddled. She landed a couple of punches that had no real effect, then absorbed several of his that did. Senses reeling, she feebly batted at his torso.

Isaiah chortled. The cuts and bumps were of no consequence. Not now. Not when he was on the verge of fulfilling his innermost desire. Pulse-pounding excitement flowed thickly through his veins. He felt more alive than he ever had, more aroused than at any time in his life. To keep her still he slugged her once more, on the jaw.

Winona's consciousness flickered like the light from a dying ember. She almost passed out. Then she felt his hands where they had no business being and indignation sparked new vitality. Bucking upward, she nearly shook him off.

"Damn you!" Isaiah fumed. He was not to be denied. A punch to her stomach left her too weak to resist. Bending, he gripped the front of her dress to rip it from her body. "Now you are mine!"

The pad of rapid footfalls twisted Isaiah around. Rushing toward him was hatred incarnate. Sunlight glimmered on a polished steel blade. He swept both arms up as the figure smashed into him, bowling him over.

"Leave her be!" Zach King screamed, beside himself with wrath. He had spied on the white men the previous afternoon and evening, then gone to sleep in the hollow of a lightning-scarred tree. Faint commotion had alerted him that something was amiss before dawn. It had stunned him when he saw his mother helping the pair.

Saddling his horse without awakening anyone else had taken longer than he reckoned. He would have liked to sneak into the cabin to fetch his bow or rifle, but he did not want his mother to gain too large a lead. Giving chase, but staying well enough back not to be spotted, he had been on a rise above the shelf when Tompkins shot Stern.

Now, incensed by the sight of the vile scum fondling his

mother, Zach fought in a bestial frenzy. They were on their knees, facing each other. He stabbed at his foe's heart, missing by a whisker when the man shifted.

Isaiah produced his own blade. "You stinking 'breed!"

Metal flashed. Zach recoiled, parried, countered, doing as his father and Shakespeare had taught him. In a knife fight it was not strength or the size of the weapon that counted, it was skill, plain and simple skill. Blade rang on blade. Zach deflected a vicious thrust at his groin, sheared at Tompkins's eye without scoring.

The white man outweighed him by a good sixty pounds, but that did not deter Zach. He would not rest until the grass was stained red by the ingrate's blood. Meeting a downward arc halfway, he reversed direction and bit the edge of his blade in deep.

Isaiah cried out. A clammy sensation spread across his right side. The wound was shallow, though, and he ignored it as he rained a flurry of blows on the youth's head and shoulders. Or tried to. For each and every one was blocked. The delay was proving costly. Out of the corner of an eye Isaiah saw the woman stir.

So did Zach, and he smiled. His mother would find a gun and end the fight. And at long last maybe she would understand the reason he had behaved as he did.

Suddenly lashing out, Isaiah drove the youth back. Then he spun and leaped, seizing Winona King as she unsteadily began to rise. Clamping his left forearm around her neck, he jabbed the tip of his knife into her shoulder just far enough to draw blood.

Zach checked his rush. Torn between his hankering to turn the white man into a sieve and worry over his ma, he wavered. "Leave her be!"

Isaiah shook Winona, gouging the knife deeper. "Do you take me for a dunce, boy? So long as I have her, you're in my power. Drop your knife and turn around. And don't dally.''

Indecision gave Zach pause. Once unarmed, he would be at the vermin's mercy. And if he were slain, where did that leave his mother? "I'll do no such thing!" he responded. "Harm her and I'll finish you.''

"You're out of your depth, child,'' Isaiah taunted. To emphasize his point, he dug a little furrow in the Shoshone's flesh.

Winona flinched and had to bite her lip in order not to cry out. Her shoulder was aflame with pain. She was groggy, her legs mush. Weakly, she tried to grasp the white man's wrist, but he shook her again, so hard her vision swam.

"Enough nonsense,'' Isaiah warned. "Boy, do as I said or I'll run this clear through.'' He drilled the cold steel inward a fraction, causing Winona to stiffen. More blood flowed.

Zach could not bear to watch his ma suffer. Flinging his knife away, he elevated his arms. "There! There! I've done as you want. Now stop hurting her!"

Mother and son shared heartfelt looks. Love filled Winona, love for this wild offspring of hers who would rather sacrifice himself than see her harmed. She had never doubted he cared. Even when they spatted, she knew that deep down he bore Nate and her a lasting affection. Here was proof. Evidence so potent it brought tears to her eyes. She longed to reach out and hug him, but she had to be content with letting her eyes mirror her sentiments.

For Zach's part, he was choked by feelings he rarely gave rein to. It made him uncomfortable to show his true emotions. He'd rather hide them. Why, exactly, he couldn't rightly say. But now, for a few brief moments, the carefree mask he usually wore was lowered—until he swiveled as the white man had commanded.

"How touching!'' Isaiah spat. They sickened him, these two, with their noble attitudes. He scanned the area for his rifle but couldn't find it. Backing up the slope, he growled, "Don't move, 'breed. Not one finger. Because if you do, your mother dies."

Winona knew Tompkins was bluffing. He wouldn't kill her until he had satisfied his perverse hunger. But she dared not shout it out or he just might cut her again. He was close to losing all semblance of self-control. She could sense it.

Zach risked a glance. His innards churned, but he was helpless so long as the man had his mother.

Where was that stinking rifle? Isaiah fumed. It had to be around there somewhere. He kicked at the high grass, throwing a tantrum. All of a sudden, remembering the squaw's weapons, he chuckled and resumed climbing.

Winona's heels dragged. She couldn't help it. Not only had she been severely beaten, but his arm was choking off her breath, making it nearly impossible for her to breathe. Gasping, she pried at his wrist, but he snarled and dug it in farther.

"Enough, you hellcat! I've taken all the nonsense from you I'm going to."

A reddish haze shrouded Isaiah's vision. His blood pounded in his ears and his chest beat to an invisible hammer. Oddly enough, he felt flushed with raw strength. Every sense was alive. He felt as if he could bend metal bars or tear a grizzly to shreds with his bare hands. *Invincible* was the word he wanted. He felt capable of besting anyone or anything.

Twisting to make sure he didn't stumble in a rut or hole, Isaiah forgot about the boy. Ten feet shy of the shelf he thought to check, and his burning wrath became an inferno. Halting, he shifted the knife to the squaw's throat and bellowed, "Where the hell did you get to, brat? I told you what would happen if you didn't listen!"

On his stomach in the high grass, Zach snaked upward. He wasn't the fool the white man believed. Tompkins was going to kill his mother eventually no matter what he did.

"May you rot in hell!" Isaiah roared. Tensing his arm to

transfix Winona, he got a grip on himself just in time. Killing her would be a waste of soft, tempting flesh. He *needed* her. But he could still use her. Hurrying higher, to the rim, he saw her pistols and her knife, and beyond them her Hawken.

Isaiah had won. Shoving Winona to her knees, he darted to the pistols and bent to scoop them up. Between his legs he glimpsed the youth, charging up onto the shelf, thinking to take him by surprise. Isaiah grinned and, whipping around, bashed the half-breed across the forehead with the barrel of a flintlock.

Zach's legs swept out from under him as the world exploded. Torment racked his noggin, rendered worse by waves of dizziness. Flat on his back, he blinked at a fluffy cloud that a second later was blotted out by the distorted features of the madman.

"I've got you now, boy, right where I want you." Fixing a pistol on the 'breed's brow, Isaiah experienced a thrill nearly as intoxicating as the thrill he would soon experience with the savage's mother.

Death stared Zach in the face. An impulse to scream nearly overcame him, but he did not submit to it. He was Stalking Coyote, son of Grizzly Killer. A Shoshone warrior. He had counted coup. He had killed Blackfeet and Bloods. He did not show fear to an enemy. He did not shriek like a terror-stricken child.

Isaiah Tompkins waited for the boy to grovel. To whine. To beg him to be spared. When it was obvious the 'breed was not going to give him the satisfaction, he brought a boot crashing down on the pup's leg. "Come on, upstart. Let me hear you squeal. Plead for mercy."

Gritting his teeth, Zach stifled another outcry. A true warrior would rather die than display weakness.

"I can't hear you," Isaiah mocked, and stomped on the youth's other leg. When that provoked no reaction, he kicked the 'breed's back and arms. Lifting his leg to start in on the

167

head, he transformed into stone at a flinty threat.

"Enough! I will send you straight to your fiery Hell, white man, if you hurt my son again."

Off balance, Isaiah bent his neck. The Shoshone woman had reclaimed her rifle and was pointing it at his shoulder blades. He entertained no doubts whatsoever that she would shoot. The wonder of it was that she hadn't already.

Winona would have. She wanted to kill this human abomination, to rid the earth of his foul presence. But his cocked pistol was pointed at her son, and she had seen men squeeze a trigger in sheer reflex at the moment of death. "Now it is your turn to put down your weapons. Do it very slowly, Mr. Tompkins. Slower than you have ever done anything."

Isaiah was not about to comply. The setbacks were aggravating, but they only delayed the inevitable. He *would* have her. He was not to be denied. Unexpectedly training the other flintlock on her, he barked, "Don't be ridiculous, my dear. What we have here is a stalemate. If you shoot me, I'll shoot the two of you. Are you a gambler? Will you risk your brat's life?"

What else was a parent to do? Winona began to lower the Hawken. Tompkins had beaten her.

"Finally!" Isaiah crowed. The heady spice of triumph filled him with elation. He would shoot the 'breed, have his way with the squaw, and be on his way before any of their family or friends arrived. By riding the horses in relays he would outdistance all pursuers. He had done it!

In that grand and glorious moment Isaiah heard the crash of undergrowth bordering the shelf. He looked up as an apparition burst into the open, a filthy buckskin-clad apparition in an equally filthy beaver hat. Mounted astride a lathered black stallion, the rider bore down on him.

"You!" Isaiah exclaimed.

Winona's hand flew to her throat. "Husband!"

Zach was on an elbow, gawking. "Pa?" he declared.

Nate King had eyes only for the New Yorker. He had reached the cabin an hour and a half before to find an upset Shakespeare and the note his wife had left. Without delay he'd set out again, in his haste neglecting to switch mounts. He'd about ridden the stallion into the ground when he spied the body of Rufus Stern off through the trees—and seen Isaiah threatening his wife and son.

Shooting the greenhorn never entered Nate's mind. Reversing his grip on his Hawken, he held it like a club, controlling the stallion by his legs alone.

Isaiah Tompkins snapped off a hasty shot. And missed. Throwing the spent pistol down, he clasped the other flintlock in both hands. He wouldn't make the same mistake twice. He took deliberate aim at the mountain man's head.

Winona brought her rifle up. The hammer had been cocked. A stroke of her finger would end it. Then her husband hollered—a rumbling "No!"—and she honored his request by not firing.

Zach shoved into a crouch, fearful his pa was about to be slain. "Try me!" he yelled, flinging himself at the lecher.

Too many! Isaiah's mind screamed. The woman had a rifle. The boy was charging. The father was almost on top of him. Which one should he kill first? In that split second of delay he sowed his undoing.

For in a thunder of hooves Nate King was on his quarry. Broad shoulders rippled, cleaving the air with the Hawken's heavy stock—the air and more, for the thick wood splintered Isaiah Tompkins's skull as if his cranium were an overripe melon.

The last sight Isaiah had was of strangely dark blood flowing over his eyes. The last sound he heard was his own rattling wail. The last sensation he felt was of falling into a mysterious void that gaped like the maw of a gigantic nether beast, of falling and falling without end toward a demonic shape lurking below.

In a spray of grass Nate reined up and vaulted down. His wife was in his arms in an instant, her warm lips against his neck. His son paused, but Nate beckoned and held them both close. "You're safe," he whispered in gratitude. "You're alive."

For the longest while sniffling was the only sound. When, at length, Winona stepped back, the three of them moved to the body of Rufus Stern. "He was a decent man," she said.

"We should make sure the scavengers do not get him."

"We will," Nate pledged.

"One other thing, husband, if you please," Winona said, cracking a smile.

"Anything."

"The next time you want to invite company home, check with me first."

#45
WILDERNESS
IN CRUEL CLUTCHES
David Thompson

Zach King, son of legendary mountain man Nate King, is at home in the harshest terrain of the Rockies. But nothing can prepare him for the perils of civilization. Locked in a deadly game of cat-and-mouse with his sister's kidnapper, Zach wends his way through the streets of New Orleans like the seasoned hunter he is. Yet this is not the wild, and the trappings of society offer his prey only more places to hide. Dodging fists, knives, bullets and even jail, Zach will have to adjust to his new territory quickly—his sister's life depends on it.

MAX BRAND®

JOKERS EXTRA WILD

Anyone making a living on the rough frontier took a bit of a gamble, but no Western writer knows how to up the ante like Max Brand. In "Speedy—Deputy," the title character racks up big winnings on the roulette wheel, but that won't help him when he's named deputy sheriff—a job where no one's lasted more than a week. "Satan's Gun Rider" continues the adventures of the infamous Sleeper, whose name belies his ability to bury a knife to the hilt with just a flick of his wrist. And in the title story, a professional gambler inherits a ring that lands him in a world of trouble.

PETER DAWSON

FORGOTTEN DESTINY

Over the decades, Peter Dawson has become well known for his classic style and action-packed stories. This volume collects in paperback for the first time three of his most popular novellas—all of which embody the dramatic struggles that made the American frontier unique and its people the stuff of legends. The title story finds Bill Duncan on the way to help his friend Tom Bostwick avoid foreclosure. But along the trail, Bill's shot, robbed and left for dead—with no memory of who he is or where he was going. Only Tom can help him, but a crooked sheriff plans to use Bill as a pawn to get the Bostwick spread for himself. Can Bill remember whose side he's supposed to be on before it's too late?

LOREN ZANE GREY

AMBUSH FOR LASSITER

Framed for a murder they didn't commit, Lassiter and his best pal Borling are looking at twenty-five years of hard time in the most notorious prison of the West. In a daring move, they make a break for freedom—only to be double-crossed at the last minute. Lassiter ends up in solitary confinement, but Borling takes a bullet to the back. When at last Lassiter makes it out, there's only one thing on his mind: vengeance.

RIDERS TO MOON ROCK

ANDREW J. FENADY

Like the stony peak of Moon Rock, Shannon knew what it was to be beaten by the elements yet stand tall and proud despite numerous storms. Shannon never quite fit in with the rest of the world. First raised by Kiowas and then taken in by a wealthy rancher, he found himself rejected by society time after time. Everything he ever wanted was always just out of his grasp, kept away by those who resented his upbringing and feared his ambition. But Shannon is determined to wait out his enemies and take what is rightfully his—no matter what the cost.